Wendy Brandmark

He Runs the Moon
Tales from the Cities

Holland Park Press London

Published by Holland Park Press 2016

Copyright © Wendy Brandmark 2016

First Edition

A CIP catalogue record for this book is
available from The British Library

ISBN 978-1-907320-60-6

Cover designed by Reactive Graphics

Printed and bound by
CIP Group (UK) Ltd, Croydon CR0 4YY

www.hollandparkpress.co.uk

He Runs the Moon is a collection of wonderfully atmospheric stories of life in the rundown Capitol Hill area of Denver in the early 1970s, in the Bronx, New York during the 1950s & 60s and in the Boston and Cambridge area in the 1970s.

Brandmark, a great storyteller in the American tradition, draws you in. Take the Denver stories which form a narrative of a Gothic city populated by people who feel they don't quite belong. In one story female creative writing students are all secretly in love with their professor but does he really register them at all? Can a girl become emotional attached to a temperamental red Mustang? You bet, especially after her boyfriend leaves for Los Angeles.

Figures from the 'old world' haunt the children and adults in the Jewish community of New York City. A troubled granny with a head that is bothering her, and the 'witch' in the basement flat, with strange dark marks on her lower arm, who comes to the rescue when a child is lost.

In the Boston tales characters piece together dreams from the fragments of their lives. Be transported, for example, to the world of an obsessive dental hygienist, and the occupational hazards of sharing rooms in a dull green clapboard house which seemed to pitch and heave.

In memory of my sister Sandy and our Bronx childhood

CONTENTS

THE DENVER OPHELIA

THE BORDERS OF MY SELF

HE RUNS THE MOON

THE DENVER OPHELIA

Cinderella went to her mother's grave beneath the hazel tree and cried: 'Shiver and quiver, little tree, Silver and gold throw down over me.' The bird threw a gold and silver dress down to her.

From *Grimm's Fairy Tales*

Ruthie buys her clothes off the backs of other women. I say, 'My mother would die if she saw me in here.'

'But she is.' Ruthie puts up her hands. 'Dead.'

'Can you be nicer about it? It's only been a year.'

We're in the death throes, the last stages of writing our dissertations, what she calls 'our dissembling'. She's been here for five years finishing.

After hours spent gleaning and writing, we meet up in the afternoon beneath a sky blue as the virgin's dress. Dry blue with never a tear. 'Heaven's hell,' Ruthie calls Denver.

She drags me to the Salvation Army store on Colfax, a wide, loud street where cowboys still roam. The store smells of sweat and disaster. I keep to the doorway while Ruthie rummages, then emerges with something muddy colored. Even her underwear comes from there.

Then we eat lemon meringue pie and try on hats at May D & F, Denver's genteel department store. The hats are my idea, big floppy things in white veil or straw. I laugh with her when we look in the mirror together, but secretly love myself in these hats rising and dipping around my face like huge flowers and me the center.

'Can you even imagine wearing this back home?' She turns from the mirror in a hat with a cascade of silk daisies. The brim seems to point to her big nose and firm chin.

She stares at me in my large white veil floppy, and her face grows sad. 'You look cute in that.'

13

'Cute' is not what I want to hear, so I shrug off the compliment.

'Really,' she says.

We've been lured to this shadowless city by fellowships. She's Manhattan, I'm Queens; she lords it over me because Queens is not really the city, but a suburb aching to join the clamour of downtown. Even so Ruthie has made me her best friend. I must not forget her voice breaking through the hard dry days of my first year here.

But there are secrets she will never know about me. I keep a postcard in my bedroom of a woman drowning in a riverbed of flowers, so peaceful now that she's given up the struggle. Lydia, who shares our office, gave it to me after I admired her print of Chatterton on his deathbed beneath a casement window.

'It calms me just to look at him,' she said. A week later I found Ophelia on my desk. I had to take her home because if Ruthie ever saw, she would say how decadent.

Lydia is one these graduate student prairie women who wear long dresses and boots and talk about pregnancy dreams. I have never had a pregnancy dream, but in the night my mother stands on the other side of the door pounding. I wake to silence and then I know what Lydia means about the calm. Ophelia, Chatterton. In their dying hearts is the finality I long for.

I have another secret from Ruthie which I will never share with anyone. I am in love with Professor Levine. What shames me is not that he's my advisor or that he's married, or even that he's twice my age and probably shorter than me. How could anyone but the most pathetic fall for a skinny, white-faced man with a pendulous nose and wisps of eyebrows above his Denver blues? That's what I call them for they are relentless. When he sneers at my little ideas and gives me one of his sideways grins, I feel elated, his sarcasm like an embrace. I imagine us in bed together, me caressing his bald head, his arms around me, the two of us like skeletons dancing; for I am, in my mother's words, 'a bony wonder'.

Ruthie makes do with men. She sees John, a big guy with a beard down to his waist who wanders around the department telling everyone he's becoming a Jew. She doesn't mind him using her to gain entrance to the 'land of Canaan' as he calls it, or his stink.

We're on one of our jaunts down Colfax. Ruthie's just bought a black full-length slip she pulled out of one of the boxes of underwear at the Salvation Army. She came right out of the dressing room wearing it in front of all the creepy guys. Just to show me. They took no notice, the downcast ones picking through racks of brown winter jackets. Only the young guy trying on stilettos grinned at her. I'm wondering when Ruthie will wear her slip since I've never seen her in a dress.

Still she's feeling good. When I pause in front of a store I haven't noticed before, a tiny place which catches me because in the window is my Ophelia, a full size mannequin dressed in white and covered in flowers, Ruthie agrees to go in even though she's ready for cake.

Inside the tiny dark room a young woman in a floppy straw hat sits at a high counter working on something. She puts whatever it is away and gives us a slow smile full of misshapen teeth. I sniff the air but smell only velvet and the incense the woman is burning near her busy fingers.

Ruthie does a bit of flicking. 'Will you look at the price of this?'

'Are these second hand?' she asks.

'Second or third,' the woman says.

Ruthie whispers to me that this is a resale store where women try to make a profit from fancy dresses they've only worn once. She doesn't want to stay.

I imagine myself in one of the gowns walking into Professor Levine's office, my skin as white as his against black velvet. I shake my head free of this for I have not bought a dress or skirt for years. Skirts come up short and dresses hang on me, wrinkling where they should fit, folds of material over my emptiness. Tears come to my eyes. I will look like a badly clothed scarecrow.

Ruthie sighs. She says she'll wait outside. 'Precious, so precious,' she whispers loud enough for the woman to hear. But I know why she hates it in here. She has to feel like a discoverer in the murk of other people.

I have a session with Professor Levine the next day. For once he does not criticize what I have written, but says something which confuses me. I haven't told Ruthie that I'm working on the final draft of my dissertation and can see the end. She's been stuck for two years on her final chapter. She goes to Levine only to whine.

He's sitting there in an open white shirt, sleeves half rolled up, his legs stretched out. His smile is almost friendly though I take care with what I say for he loves to make fun of me and then turn cold when I too become playful. I was almost late because I dressed for him and today I wasn't right in anything. I settled for my boy jeans and black tee shirt, hoping the sight of my pale face with hair tied at the neck will make him think Pre-Raphaelite because I'm certain this is the look he craves, a sad-eyed reed woman like the belle dame of his favorite poet. But he doesn't notice me as a woman. I'm just a mind to him and not a very good one.

Suddenly he's talking about Jane Eyre's quest for transcendence, and I'm thinking that I would have to insert whole sections, bringing the dissertation up from its dungeons of desire. 'But that means changing everything, doesn't it?'

He gives me one of his kryptonite looks, eyes fixed on me, thin mouth quivering because he's poised to make one of his sharp little comments which will hurt me, but then in retrospect have a pleasing tenderness, like a healing wound which tickles. He says nothing, only shrugs and indicates our time is over. 'I suppose I could do it,' I say, but he's looking out the window as if I'm already gone.

In the afternoon Ruthie wants to go out for cakes as usual, but I'm longing to get back to the tiny store. I can't have her moaning around me while I try on. I don't want a bargain; I want to spend myself in that store so when I emerge I will be like that figure of glory Professor Levine dreams of.

I go along with Ruthie and then after we part, I circle around the streets of Capitol Hill where the flat city rises and falls, and come back to Colfax. Why I must hide my return to this store from her I don't understand. At first I don't find the store and think that maybe it appeared just on that day like *Brigadoon*. Then I see Ophelia and notice for the first time the store's name, written in purple: *Chrysalis*.

The same woman bent over her work looks up. She doesn't remember me. Her pale lashes, the weedy hair sticking out of her hat and her crooked teeth make me feel dizzy. There's something not right about her, as if she has been broken up and re-formed with some of the wrong pieces.

I try on a black kaftan dress, but it swamps me in the little curtained changing room. I put on a green velvet empire waist, but its short tight puffy sleeves make my arms look like spindles. All the other dresses are too short. I sit down on the little stool and hear my mother wonder what a sensible girl like me wants with an old-fashioned floor-length velvet dress. I put on my tee shirt and sneakers, my boy jeans.

The woman watches me hang up the dresses.

'Have you been lucky?' she asks.

I shake my head. 'None of them fit. I'm sorry.' Why should I be sorry? Always.

I turn away and begin pulling open the door when I hear her call out 'wait' in a peculiar hoarse way like a boy whose voice has just broken.

She goes to a back room. It seems a long time before she returns with an armful of scarlet velvet and shakes out a dress which makes me hungry. She gives no explanation about why it was in the back. I decide it just arrived, some woman finally deciding to give up.

I come out to stand before the mirror. The long puffy sleeves shield my thin arms. The skirt falls in waves from the fitted low-cut bodice which makes me look full. I turn and turn again trying to see myself from all sides. It is as if the dress were made for me, even to the length. It just touches my heels, its soft velvet like the hands of a fairy godmother.

17

Back in the changing room I bring the velvet up to my face and sniff. No sweat or stale sadness of Ruth's Salvation Army, but something else. I sniff again and decide it is the incense the woman burns. Someone has bought this dress and not worn it even once.

The dress costs more than what I spend on a week's food, but I will have it. I will be like those lanky prairie women whose skirts trail over hiking boots. I will come into Professor Levine's office like a vision.

The dress hangs like a woman in a swoon over my arm. She reaches for it. I can't bear to see the velvet slipped into one of these wrinkled paper bags Ruthie comes away with from the Salvation Army, but she folds the dress and carefully wraps a length of purple tissue around it.

Next week I'm in my cubicle, my head down on a pile of freshman papers, when Ruthie gives me a poke. She wants me to come cake eating with her in the afternoon, but I've got Professor Levine at two. It was the only appointment left.

'Again? You saw him a minute ago.'

'You know he's asking for changes.'

She doesn't buy this. 'How many times do you see him?'

'Just once a week.'

'For God's sake Cathy, why d'you see him so much?'

'Maybe it's not once a week.'

She looks at me: 'You're holding something from me?'

'You've been here longer. I'm just getting going.'

We have a strange moment when she keeps trying to get me to look her straight in the eyes but I don't.

'Stay on the bridge then,' she says turning her back.

Ruthie is right. I see him too much and the last time he looked at me not with irritation but curiosity: what does she want, this girl? For he is innocent when it comes to sex. I'm sure he has only ever slept with his high-bosomed, haughty wife.

I make up questions for him, questions and questions of questions. He tells me I need to read this one and that one.

All the time I'm thinking of the scarlet dress like it is my sad daughter.

So why do I go back to the store again? Ruthie at least wears the clothes she buys. Ophelia is still in the window and incense burns at the grey-eyed woman's side as she does her close work. I turn to the other racks of long dresses, all of flimsy material: silk, organdie, lace. Again I find nothing to fit and again the woman brings out a long dress just waiting for me, of white lacy material like a bride's nightgown. It fits around my body like seaweed. I hear someone, could be Ruthie, could be my mother, cry out when I bring the dress up to the counter and take out my wallet. 'Never,' they cry like a Greek chorus, 'never will you wear this.'

'It's amazing,' I say to grey eyes, 'it fits me to a T.'

She smiles at me, blinking her long colorless lashes.

It's a mistake to meet Ruthie after that with the purple tissue paper bundle in my arms. She's so nosy. But I couldn't keep saying no to her. Even though her pronouncements on everyone else drive them away, she's my only real friend out here, the one who when I'm shaking with flu, will come with her own spoon and cough medicine.

She's standing outside the Salvation Army with one of their wrinkled bags.

'What'd you get?' I ask.

'What you get?' Already she's torn the tissue paper.

'Hey.' I grab it back and hold it close to my chest.

'You've been there again, haven't you? You realize what a rip-off they are? Used clothing they're selling like new.'

'They're antique,' I say.

She pulls out of her bag a long burgundy dress with embroidery across the front, the ethnic kind which just hangs and you know no one in India or Istanbul would ever wear it. She's still pulling stuff out: a satiny blouse which feels synthetic, a black blazer with padded shoulders. I don't say that I can see the shine on one of the sleeves.

'You had a success,' I say.

'All this for ten dollars. How much did that cost you?'

19

'So good for you.'

'Tell me.' She pulls at the tissue paper and manages to rip it so the dress is exposed in all its laciness.

'What is with you?'

'Should we try on hats? Or do you want to eat something?'

'I wanna know what you're buying this for.'

I think for a moment that she suspects about Professor Levine, and blush to think of myself in love with the man of bone.

'I'm going to a wedding.'

She takes this in then says: 'You're wearing white to a wedding?'

'Oh. I forgot.'

Ruthie hunches up one shoulder and turns from me. I take her arm. 'C'mon Ruthie. Let's eat cake.'

'Don't bullshit me, Cathy. Ever.'

I calm her at May D & F talking about her favorite subject, the prairie women.

'Don't you go becoming like them,' she says.

'What do you mean?'

'Just don't get all vague. Like Lydia.'

She looks at me almost tenderly, and I see she worries about losing me, me more than grey beard John.

We share a slice of seven-layer cake and go off to the hat department. The floppys of summer have gone. We're trying on fur hats and berets. Ruthie scoops up her long hair and tucks it all into a black beret, then turns to me. I hope she doesn't notice the shock on my face. I'm looking not at her, but Professor Levine: the same long white face, big nose, even the eyes. I don't say anything, of course I don't say anything. She keeps staring at herself in the mirror and laughing. I'm sick with looking at her, reach over and pull at the beret till her brown mane straggles down her long neck.

'Hey.' She turns from the mirror. 'Why'd you do that, I was having fun.'

'You looked like a jerk.'

I sit at my desk in my shoebox bedroom, my hands in folds of scarlet velvet. I feel a wild joy every time I put it on. Sometimes I fear such joy as if the dress will flame up and consume me. Yesterday it was the turn of the wedding dress as I typed. Still perfumed not with incense I've decided, but some musk enduring even after I have washed it.

'Something's going on.' Ruthie talks while she eats her coconut custard pie. She's seen Lydia go into Professor Levine's office and emerge hours later.

'How do you know? She could've come and gone and then gone back again. You didn't hang around there.'

'I did actually.'

'But he…' I do that funny thing where my throat ends up in my mouth and I have to swallow before I can speak.

'Yeah, I know, he's pure. But what's she doing?'

'Talking. She told me she's run into a block.'

'Her head maybe.'

I watch her spoon the remains of the coconut custard pie into her mouth and think of Lydia's moon face rising above the flat land. You could never know these prairie women. Maybe Lydia had loves as strange as her Chatterton.

I can't sit still anymore.

'What about your éclair?'

We both look at the long lean pastry. Ruthie begins to laugh.

'I'm going home.'

'So go. I'm fed up with hats anyway.'

But I walk to my store. I rummage around, then stand before the young woman about to say what I always say. She's hard at work, head bent, so very occupied that she does not notice me. I look down to see her long fingers pasting silver sequins on an eggshell. She's nearly finished one side and the egg lies there like a fallen moon. I am open mouthed at this so say nothing for some minutes. A shifting of my feet alerts her and she covers the egg with a length of watery silk.

'Have you been lucky?' she asks.

'No not this time. But maybe you have something else.'

At this point she will bring out something, I know she will. But she shakes her head.

'She hasn't come in. Not this week. Not last.'

I stare at her, her grey eyes and wispy hair. Ruthie was right. She was not born a woman.

'You mean they're all from one person? Well I figured. They both fit so perfectly.' Only I hadn't. Nobody had ever owned the dresses before me, and even I could not possess them.

'The only problem with them is the smell. Not a bad smell, but I can't get rid of it.'

She looks at me sadly.

Maybe she's died, the woman who has given me her velvet and lace.

'Has she, I mean do you think…?' I choke even though I'm smiling, so the sentence never finishes. I'm wearing ghost's clothes, smelling her sweetness from the grave.

It's then I smell the perfume again and realize it comes from her. For once she's not burning incense and I can smell her or him or whoever.

'She doesn't come,' she repeats.

I can see she longs to get back to her eggshell.

That night I dream again about my mother. We're in our yard. She tells me to get the apple from the very top of the tree. Only that one will do. I climb for hours, pushing myself through dense branches which tear at my face. When I'm clear, I reach for the apple, but close my hand on a cloud, a seed flower.

My next appointment with Professor Levine is Friday. In those days before, I keep to my apartment. I don't even show up for my office hour with my freshman students on Wednesday. Because I don't want to meet Lydia, see her dresses trailing into Levine's office, moon-face Lydia, Ophelia of the prairie.

On Friday morning I'm in my jeans and black shirt typing at the little desk. I'm supposed to see him at eleven. At least I know that Lydia won't be there before me. She writes at night, then sleeps until lunch, like some wraith, some sister of Dracula.

I smell again the perfume and am drawn to my dresses. The white lace clings as nothing has ever done before. As I let my hair down I see myself lying face upwards in a lake, Professor Levine reaching into the wet leaves for me.

I know I will be back in my jeans again before I leave, and the bride dress will wait for me with its smell of the boy woman. 'Sometimes a dress finds you,' she said when I bought the last one. I whisper her words to myself.

I'm pulling on my boots, going out the door with my books in my arms because I couldn't wear a knapsack with the dress. The boots yes, Lydia would wear them with a ball gown, but never the knapsack. She carries her books in beaded bags which hang from her flat arms.

All the way down Capitol Hill to Broadway I know I'll go home. I could call the department secretary to say I'm too sick to see him. Even on the bus, crossing my legs in the stretchy lace, I know I won't see him like this. But the dress carries me above even the plateau on which the city rests, for I have lost the substance of myself, my bones filled with light.

I'm walking up to my office, lifting my dress as I mount each step. When I look inside the room I share with four others, I see no one. I creep to my cubicle to wait. Then I hear steps and see a long braid of hair. If I slump down she might not see me, for her cubicle is at the other end of the room.

But I know she will come looking. As I hear her moving towards me, I fold my arms over my chest and look down at some student papers.

Ruthie starts to speak then stops. 'What are you?'

I will her not to laugh at me, but she does not even smile.

'I'm late,' I say, though I have minutes.

She continues to stare at me. Something has happened to her mouth because it doesn't speak. Then she asks, 'Late for who? Just who?'

'Who do you think?'

'You're seeing him in that?'

I look down at myself.

'You're having a thing with him.'

'Are you kidding?'

'Tell me. I wanna know. I need to know.' Her lips are actually trembling.

'Why should I? With him?' I start to say 'he's so ugly', but I can't.

She looks angry. Maybe she knows how much she resembles Levine. 'You are. I know you are. I can see right through you.'

The lacy material hides nothing not even my nipples.

'Why didn't you tell me? You could have. You don't really care for him.'

I raise both my hands high to plead my innocence and feel the thin material tear. 'Shit.'

'All along I thought he was pure and that's why I never really tried though I wanted to. So much. Just offer myself.'

Is it shock or something else making me dizzy? I regain myself and look at her sad face.

'That's why I avoided him. It was breaking my heart.'

'Ruthie, I never. Believe me.'

She sits down and puts her hands over her face.

I put my arm around her. 'I thought I was the only one. But believe me, he never.'

She wipes her eyes and nose and gives me one of her looks which almost relieves me for it is Ruthie I see again.

'Are you kidding? There's not one woman in the department who doesn't want him. Just to have him sneer at you. It's unbearable.' She wipes her eyes. 'You got a tissue?'

I shake my head.

'So gimme something.' She points to my pad of notes. I tear out the first page. 'Hey that has writing on it,' she says.

I shrug. 'Go on. I don't need it.' It's a page of questions I was planning to ask him carefully formed so that he could not look beneath the words and see me. I watch her blow her nose in it.

'You're really not?' She stares hard into my face. 'So why the fuck are you dressed for it?'

To this I say nothing. I smell again the sharp sweetness like a scent of madness. I want to rip off what little I have on.

We hear laughter from the direction of his office. The moon face of Lydia passes through the doorway beyond our cubicles. Ruthie just stares, then she whispers: 'Her.'

She'll fill him with her emptiness.

'Can I wear your jacket? Just to go in there?'

'Fool,' Ruthie says, but she gives it to me, the one with the padded shoulders and second hand shine. With the jacket buttoned up, he'll see only a skirt of lace.

'Wish me luck.' Why did I say that? I can't tell her I'm handing in my last chapter.

She gives me one of her Manhattan up and down stares. 'You look like a jerk.'

I just stand there waiting.

'So good luck already. You want me to spit on you like my grandmother does?'

As I turn I hear her whisper so low that I don't know if she's speaking to me or herself: 'I'll miss you.'

I'm in there talking to his silence. There's something naked about his face; the eyes once so fearsome seem mere lights. I hand him the pages I typed in my scarlet dress, in my lace.

'I worked transcendence into it,' I say.

He smiles but not at me, and I think how many times I've cradled that death's head.

I'm circling around Colfax. Not returning, not ever, but when I shut my eyes the boy woman holds out a dress cut from the Denver sky.

In the window of *Chrysalis* Ophelia has fallen from her bed and lost all her flowers. She's not a mannequin after all, but a big doll whose lashed eyes have opened. Words shape themselves in the hollow of her mouth. 'She comes again,' I hear her say.

And I make for home.

I was never one of these people who wear their car around them like some adorable child. Even in the early days when I drove down Broadway trying to sing to the radio, elbow on the window, curls blowing, just like everyone else in a car, even then my legs trembled. And the car pulled this way and that, shaking when I speeded up. I never thought of it as old though the car was in its dotage. Because it was bright red and still shiny. A Mustang. And the car loved its long sleek shape, like youth itself.

'So big,' I said when the owner drove up. I'd imagined myself ensconced in one of these little bug cars.

'Not really,' Jeff said, brushing his hand along the hood and then smiling at me, his green eyes bright with desire.

I could see he had fallen for the Mustang, and I put my hand deep in my pocket to pay for all that was wrong with it. He wanted to go up into the mountains so we got new brake shoes and tires. Days after he left for Los Angeles the battery went. And then the problems became chronic. It was a car which took at least ten minutes to start.

We had come west together from New York City to teach at colleges we'd never heard of. Let's face it I'd say to him, they'll never have us back again, they the nobility of the East coast who had spawned and then abandoned me.

'Why care?' Jeff said. Because he was going home. He threw down his doctorate in philosophy and on the basis of one video about chicken hearts talking, took a job teaching film in the rotten core of LA.

I saw myself surrounded by verdant mountains with glittering streams, but as the plane circled and circled I looked out to see the towers of Denver rise out of the dry plain. I was stuck there in an English Department headed by a short Texan who wore a cravat and goatee and said 'Howdy'. At the beginning of the semester, the faculty held their 'jamboree' at

27

a ranch house where one of the professors lived with her pet horse, and where I was nearly squashed by the department's bulky poet. He said by way of an apology, 'Better watch out little girl or I'll step on you.' I drove the Mustang back in the dark, the mountains like silent men watching my descent into the city.

When I told Jeff over the phone about the Mustang's behavior, he said, 'It's a good car.'

I realized that despite his long experience with driving he knew nothing about cars. He had grown up on the LA freeways; cars for him were like horses he could mount and ride away, and it didn't matter if tomorrow his stallion couldn't carry him, he'd find another.

'You could sell it.'

'I don't believe you. After you pushed me to buy it. You said I had to have a car here. You said.'

'You trade in. One used car for another.'

'Can you see me in a used car lot? I'd end up like Jack in the beanstalk with only beans.'

He laughed his rollicking laugh. He'd gone California, as if the sunlight had faded the Eastern angst and he was golden again. Only I carried New York around these brilliant streets, still in my Jewish skin of dread and deep thinking. The blue sky was like an eye of doom on my special little darkness.

Jeff always said of me, 'She knows how to ride the trains,' because I'd learned to drive late and my heart did a little dance when I had to speed up. At twenty-six I was ashamed to say that this was my first car and maybe had I stayed in Brooklyn I would never have had a car. How I missed the New York subway, the heavy filthiness of it, the iron roar which could crush your heart, the dark in moments when the lights failed and you were left alone with strangers.

Denver had no subway, and as Jeff said only odd souls rode the few buses. These figures I saw at the wavering edges of my vision whenever I walked up Colfax or sat in White Spot with coffee. I didn't know till later that I could be one of them and be happy.

28

I dreaded mornings, the Mustang waiting for me to give it life in the bright street. Again and again I tried the ignition till its slack blood quickened and I could be on my way.

I complained about the Mustang on the phone to Jeff at Thanksgiving but he seemed not to hear. When I asked was he coming to Denver for Christmas he kept talking about the comfort of nothingness. He was making a film about two people who disappeared slowly until only their breath was left.

'Will you stop this bull. You said one of us should go to the other.'

There was a long pause. I scratched the receiver.

'What's that?'

'What's what?'

Another pause and then I said, 'So I'll see you when.'

'Aren't you going to your folks?'

'I only have one folks. A mother in Brooklyn. Remember?'

'Hey just lighten.'

'If I go to New York I won't come back. I just will not be able to bear it.'

'That bad?'

Suddenly I could smell him naked, his golden skin moist and warm, like some god who came not from the clouds but the fragrant earth. I really couldn't speak at that moment for fear that I might start sobbing.

'So maybe stay there.'

I got off the phone and began to pace. I lived in a one-room flat so crammed with furniture that I had to move cautiously, as if the royal blue sofa and the melamine table found me burdensome. I looked out the window at my Mustang. We were alone. Jeff had got me with car and left me.

I did go to Brooklyn for Christmas break because Jeff couldn't make up his mind where he wanted to be. The morning I left, the Mustang was parked in the street, its hood streaked with snow. When I looked back, I thought for the first time the car was showing its age. It had a neglected look, the paintwork no longer gleaming. You could see more clearly the rust its former owner had tried to cover up.

29

The janitor in my building promised to start it up every few days while I was away. I thought the car might die and then I would be rid of it. I felt melancholic all the way to the airport on the bus which wound its way round and round the suburbs of Denver.

But somehow the Mustang survived the winter.

During the second semester I discovered other New Yorkers in the English Department. One of them was a gaunt Joyce man from the Bronx. The other was a beefy guy of middle age who wore chunky cardigans and wrote novels about himself having poignant sex with young women. He was a fellow Jew, the first I met in Denver which is maybe why I said to him, 'I can't acclimate. How do you stand it?'

His mouth turned up in sneer. 'Then go back if it's so bad.'

The Joyce man had an unexpectedly deep voice and his long lined face looked like it had taken a million drinks. I told him about the car.

'You got a Mustang?'

I couldn't see it was that funny certainly not for him to break off into coughing.

'Yeah but I don't want to have it anymore.'

He had his eye on me this taper of a man.

It was in the full glare of a Denver spring that the Mustang had the first of its episodes. 'C'mon,' I said, but the sound when I turned the ignition was not good. The cars behind me began to honk, one after the other as if I willfully stopped in the middle of the road. Finally they began driving around me, the men with their arms half out the windows. I got out and pulled up the hood as I had seen others do. As I stared into the inner workings of my Mustang, a man appeared from one of the cars, a florid fellow who grinned at me.

'What's the problem?'

'I don't know. It never happened before.'

'That's what they all say.' He bent over it and did something to the engine, then asked me to go back into the car and try to

30

start it. It worked and I blessed him. But as I drove on I blushed for the nakedness of my Mustang thrown open for all to see.

The car had these little breakdowns several times over the next few weeks, but a man always appeared who could revive it. One day I got lost and turned down a street I never thought Denver had, dabbled with shadows from large ancient trees, and people actually strolling on the wide sidewalks with stores you'd find in Brooklyn: Emily's beads, One Hand Books, even an old fashioned candy store.

The car seemed as transfixed as me. We were ambling down the road when the engine began to stutter. As usual I pulled up the hood and then stood there waiting. A young guy with hair down his back sauntered by, drawled 'hiyah howdy' but didn't stop. I got so far as touching what I thought were the spark plugs when she emerged from the bead shop, a woman with shiny black hair and one feather earring. She looked like an Indian with her upright bearing and fringed jacket. She went right to work.

I stood watching her. 'I wish I could get rid of it. How I wish. It's such a pain in the neck.' I was reminded of how my mother used to speak of me when I pulled at her sleeve to go my way, my way.

She smiled at me. 'You tried selling it?'

I shook my head. Nobody would want this car.

'You clean it up. You'll see. Someone will want this shape, someone will.'

I almost said 'What about you?' but I could see it wasn't her sort of car.

She waved to me as I started to drive down the street. I suddenly thought I should get her telephone number. She might want it after all, but more, much more I wanted to see her again. When I turned around she was gone. I imagined her astride a motorcycle or a high black stallion.

She put the idea in my head: I could just sell. Even though I knew how difficult it would be without a car, each morning as I worked over the ignition, I thought I don't have to own you anymore.

31

A week later I took it to the supermarket. At the cash register the store manager offered me a free tub of ice cream if I let him check my receipt. I reckoned maybe my luck was changing.

I took the streets one after the other, singing 'Sunshine on my shoulder'. As I slowed down just before Colfax, the Mustang stalled and even began smoking. I got out fast and opened the hood. The cars went by and by and there I was with my carton of good luck chocolate ice cream quietly melting. I thought of the black-haired woman with the feather earring galloping down Colfax towards me.

Then he appeared, a short tight man with sunglasses, his sleeves rolled up. I said the usual things about wanting to rid myself of the car, but he said nothing. He fiddled with the inside, told me to start it. He tried again but it still wouldn't start and he hit the side of the car with the flat of his hand. 'Bitch.'

When he got it going, he came round to the window. 'I'll give you $200. You got no engine.'

'Then why?'

'The shape. My daughter'll like the shape. I'll gut it.'

He looked like he'd never had a daughter. I took the card he gave me. 'That's not much,' I said.

'If you can't get more,' he said.

We rolled along after that, me in a pensive mood. I whispered, 'Don't worry. I won't give you to him.'

But something happened to me. I began to fear getting into the car because I would never know how or where it would fail.

I put an ad in the *Rocky Mountain News*, a simple two liner which said nothing about the Mustang's problems. But they were not fooled. The ex-policeman, who left his epileptic wife with me as security while he drove the Mustang, came back with a pale shocked look. 'Don't want to upset her,' he whispered looking at his wife who had said nothing as she sat on my blue sofa, 'but you got a blowed motor.' Another man took one look at the oil leaking from the Mustang's decayed haunches and walked off.

I can't shake it, I told the Joyce man.

'You need a little story. People have to feel that owning this Mustang will change them.'

'In two lines?'

'Have you ever thought, maybe you don't want to sell it?'

I pondered that for a week, taking out the Mustang for judiciously short trips, always returning through the dabbled street to see if the woman with the feather earring would emerge once again from the bead shop. And the Mustang behaved as if it knew it was on trial. 'You're doing well,' I whispered, patting the wheel. 'Just don't lose your nerve.'

And then it happened on Broadway, the Mustang trembling and then dying in the starkness of that broad street with cars skidding around me. 'No,' I said, 'no, no, no.'

I phoned the small tight man that night. He didn't sound surprised or even bothered as if he picked up old Mustangs every day. 'You still want to buy it?'

'Yeah I'll gut it. I'll just gut the whole thing.'

I could see his hard arms reaching inside the Mustang's infernal engine.

I called Jeff even though we hadn't spoken for months, because he loved the Mustang. I hesitated about calling; what if he pleaded give it another chance why don't you?

But he was breezy as ever. 'It'll be your first step home if you sell her.'

I thought of the Joyce man who called the Mustang my narrative. 'No. It's a new story. Me on the buses.'

Jeff laughed. 'You'll be with your kind.'

As I stood outside beside the Mustang I imagined its past lives. It had come gleaming from the factory, the engine sharp as a baby's first cry, but even then uncertain of itself. Now the Mustang waited silently for its next owner. It had always been the patient one of the two of us.

Next morning I walked down to Broadway and waited for the bus to the university. An old woman with a large striped bag over her arm stood with me. A skinny nervy young woman joined us, books under her arm. I imagined she was a student.

I watched the cars passing so fast. Was I looking for my Mustang already gutted and moving with new speed and confidence? It would ride right by without recognizing me or even acknowledging all we had been through together. I felt light, almost insubstantial as I walked onto the bus with the others and took a window seat warmed by sunlight.

'You never really change,' Jeff had said.

I looked around; everyone was either staring out the window or deep in themselves. The nervy student was moving her lips as if rehearsing what she would say to her professor.

I imagined my hands on the wheel of the Mustang and began to make motions like a child mock driving beside her mother. I drove again but without any stalls, my hands and arms making half circles. Once a motorcycle came beside me, but it roared past before I could see the woman with the feather earring riding faster and faster till she flew up into the hot blue sky. I drove all the way to university, the Mustang's long shiny nose of a hood moving slow and steady through the stops and starts of traffic, through the bus shuddering as it paused to pick up new passengers. And then like everyone else, when I reached my stop I thanked the driver and got off.

Phil had almost refused her. His writing workshop was overbooked, but by the end of the day he felt too weary to resist. Jane Wood was not even attractive: a small tight face on the end of a bony body. He should have known what to expect; she did not plead or flatter to get into the class.

'Mr Rosen?' not even 'Professor' or the mistaken 'Doctor'. When he nodded, she shoved the registration card in his direction as if he were a machine.

Phil Rosen, the sole novelist in the English Department's tiny creative writing program, respected by his colleagues and students because he could be counted on to produce a book every two years. He wrote about married professional men having affairs with young women in New York, in Los Angeles, in Denver, where he now lived. Phil's heroes sounded much like him, although he was careful to change hair and eye coloring. His wife Carol and the wives in his novels wore identical housedresses and hung with the same unappetizing flesh. He dedicated all his novels to Carol.

The local library carried one of his books, and occasionally the back pages of the *New York Times Book Review* mentioned his newest novel. 'Life hasn't given me all its cookies,' Phil liked to say with a sneer.

But he was lucky, he told himself, to have a secure academic job in these times, lucky too to be handsome and youthful in middle age. A big man with broad shoulders, thick wavy hair, a 'Jewish Rock Hudson' one of his lovers said.

With each freshman class, he found a new mistress, usually in his writing class, for whom he was mentor, father and seducer. Although he would say they seduced him, coming to his office for criticism and the like.

Phil hardly noticed Jane Wood in the first week of class. Never very good with names, he referred to her once as 'the girl in black'. At this she said her name loudly as if he were both deaf and senile. 'Wooden faced' he thought but forgot her for a time. In the beginning Jane did not say much.

Phil was intent on another, Julie, a golden skinned blonde. He criticized her story mercilessly but at the end of the hour when he could see the beginnings of tears in Julie's bewildered eyes, he began to point out certain possibilities, room for improvement. Phil was hoping this would send her to his office before the weekend.

'What do you think of the grandmother?' he asked the class, a calculated question.

'I don't really know her. I mean her character is not really developed,' offered the ex-marine, an innocuous lad whose crew cut was growing into a hedge.

Phil nodded with satisfaction, the second week and already they were picking up his words. 'Yes I agree with that and the character traits which are given don't fit together.'

Julie's eyes remained fixed on his face the whole time.

'I wonder if this character is based on a real person?' Julie shook her head with a frankness Phil found idiotic. He wondered if her mind would turn him off physically.

Then she said it, Jane Wooden or whatever her name was. 'Why does that matter?' She had not even raised her hand.

Phil broke in immediately. 'I have never known a character to work which was not based on a real person. In all my experience,' he added humbly.

'How do you know that all of Tolstoy's characters or Joyce's were not made up?'

Phil's smile emerged a sneer. He was going to give a rational explanation with historic examples but something about her tone upset him. 'It won't work, I can tell you.'

Jane did not argue the point further. The class ended in silence. As his students stood up to leave, Phil's foot was tapping involuntarily as it did on the accelerator pedal when a driver cut out in front of him.

Afterwards he sat alone in the empty classroom, too apathetic to gather his papers and leave. When students for the next class began to file in with puzzled expressions, he was jolted to his feet.

Julie came that afternoon with her story, asking for advice. Phil felt assuaged. She had changed into a sleeveless dress; her hair was pulled back by two tiny clips but a few golden strands fell on her smooth forehead. She was charming. And had talent, if only she would stop writing about wrinkled old women.

'Write about what you know.'

Julie perked her head up as if he had coined this advice. 'It's only the second story I've written,' she said in her defence.

Yes, the course was open to anyone practically; soon he'd be getting geriatric lady writers, the ones he taught at night in his hungry days.

After their initial disagreement, Jane Wood became more vocal in class. When she wasn't arguing with his judgements on a student's story, she brought up odd questions, ones he could neither answer nor laugh off although he tried. Why didn't she smile at him, even at his poor jokes? Her small hard face incongruously framed by brown curls never relaxed.

The ex-marine brought in a story about boot camp. Two soldiers shared the local prostitute one night and found each other better company. There was just a tinge of homosexuality in the story, enough to make Phil feel broadminded about praising it.

'But I don't care about either of them. I don't like the main characters,' Jane said.

'That's not the point,' muttered the ex-marine.

Phil waited for once, hoping the rest of the class would finish her off, but they looked to him. What did they know that wasn't his?

'Do you sympathize with these men? I think we're supposed to,' Jane asked him.

No he didn't but he was not going to make it easy for her. 'I can and do admire a piece of fiction objectively for its merits.'

'But shouldn't our hearts and minds be involved?' Jane spoke with absurd sincerity.

Yes, this had been his intention as a young writer, but more and more, Phil grew disdainful of his creations.

'It's a matter of opinion.' He drew the class's attention to the next story.

At the end of that week Jane handed him three stories. At last he could pick apart her words in front of the class, regain his hold. For he was losing them gradually. There were signs. The ex-marine no longer accosted him after class with plaintive questions: 'Why do you write? How do you know when you're professional?'

Even Julie, that relationship was not progressing as rapidly as he wished. They were still at the discussing writing stage, still had not left the confines of his office. Phil grew tired of her questions which artlessly flattered him. The freshness which attracted him at the beginning, he saw as gullibility.

One quick reading revealed flaws in Jane's stories: stilted dialogue, unbelievable twists of plot. Phil felt relieved but rereading was struck by the main character in each story: a young woman who spoke to herself in a stream of brilliant images, sentence fragments. It was as if an exotic bird flew out of her mouth, that set critical mouth, singing wild, high-pitched songs.

Phil always tried to separate the student from the story in order to judge impartially, but he could not stop thinking of Jane's desires. Was she not embarrassed to reveal herself, or would she hide behind the writer's ploy? 'That is not me, not really.' A ploy with truth.

In workmanlike fashion Phil dismembered each of Jane's stories. The class was good that day, echoing his criticisms like a chorus. Phil wondered how Jane could sit there so cool and silent while the crescendo built. He waited for her protest but when it came at the next meeting, he was surprised.

Phil began by praising the interior monologue in one story about a murder. Jane stared at him with just a hint of a smile as if she scorned his conciliatory words.

'But the actions of this girl don't make sense in view of what she tells us about herself.' Phil wished she would stop trying to out-stare him. 'Someone who professes to be so passionate would not let herself be victimized so easily,' Phil concluded.

'You missed the irony,' Jane said.

'What irony?' Phil looked around the table for smiles, but found none. She does not even know the meaning of the word.

Jane began to point out sentences, whole passages with so-called double meanings; passion turned to passivity under her scrutiny.

'You see?' she demanded. One by one the students around the table began to nod their heads in agreement.

Like dogs, Phil thought.

'A story is not a puzzle. For the irony to work, it must not be obscure,' he said.

'It's not, is it?' Jane looked around.

'I don't think we need to discuss this further.' Phil felt ashamed of himself. He noticed Jane exchanging sympathetic smiles with the other students. He couldn't believe he had lost so much.

At the end of the hour, when Julie came up to ask if he had time in the afternoon for a conference, Phil turned away with a brusque 'no'. What was he doing making love to a girl of eighteen who believed everything he said, while another had challenged his right to sit in judgement?

Phil left the classroom before everyone else. His body felt cumbersome as he strode through the campus to his office. There he sat through the afternoon, trying to read student papers, picking up, putting down a new journal and finally looking out at the dead blue of the sky.

In the next office, two of his colleagues were planning the annual spring departmental outing. Phil picked up the journal again. Someone in Texas had written on the 'Ineluctable Modality of the Visible in Virginia Woolf'. He could never read this stuff. No academic he, you couldn't call yourself one without a doctorate.

Phil sat up in his chair. He was a craftsman. A wordsmith carefully creating little boxes for little people to pop their heads out of at predictable moments. Phil focused his attention out the window again.

Jane startled him appearing so suddenly on the other side of his desk. Had she watched him stare at nothing through the window, as though with sightless eyes?

'Are you busy?' she asked. Was she mocking him?

'Sit down,' he said.

'I don't agree with any of your criticisms of my stories.'

'Well, that was obvious today,' he smiled in what he hoped was a fatherly way.

'I was reading your comments; they don't really tell me anything but your opinions.'

'I can't tell you how to write your stories if that's what you mean.'

'I'm not asking that. It's just that you don't really read the stories, you have preconceived ideas. You're very opinionated in a certain way.'

'Yes I do have opinions. Students have always found my judgements very helpful.' He laughed to keep above her, to make her a child throwing tantrums.

'You dominate the whole class. Everyone's afraid to say anything.'

Phil watched her mouth as she said this, a wide mouth, 'generous' he would have described it in his earlier novels before he was sensitive to being called trite. Phil wanted to strike that mouth; it offered none of the solace for which it was intended.

And then, he felt excited – why when she was flat chested, had no ass, was a stick figure he used to draw for a woman? If only the desk wasn't in the way.

Jane was talking, but Phil could not listen for he knew he must calm himself down, look out of the window. The moment passed. He was able to deliver a mildly patronizing statement: 'Young lady, you have a chip on your shoulder. None of my students have ever complained.' He saw her flinch at this as if the charge had been made before. In her vulnerability she became desirable again.

Jane stood up awkwardly; for once she had trouble meeting his eyes. Phil moved from behind the desk as she walked toward the door. He caught her by the arm, jerking her towards him. Before he could reach her face with his lips, Jane gave him a quick push and he had to step backwards to regain his balance. She was out of the door.

Jane Wood disappeared for a week, during which Phil regained respect in the class. The small group of writers sitting around the oblong table needed him or at least they thought they did.

'The writing in here is improving,' he announced at the end of the week. They were just past mid-term when students itched to see results.

Then he asked, although he could have just as well remained silent, 'Has anyone seen Jane Wood? Is she sick, do you know?'

No reaction. If they were all compatriots, if she had talked, he would know.

The ex-marine asked, 'Is she the one with the murder story, the real skinny girl?' He shrugged his shoulders. 'I don't know her outside of class.'

No one knew where she lived. Maybe she was one of the commuter students who could not compare notes, could not organize in the dorm. And Jane seemed like a loner, probably sat home angrily nursing her wounds.

'Well, no matter. She's probably sick.' Phil dismissed her from the class communal mind. No one looked at him accusingly or much worse with amusement.

Julie approached him after class with a special favor, that he look over her revision before she sent it to the college literary rag. He took advantage of the occasion to put a fatherly arm around her. They made an appointment for next week, late in the day, a time when Phil knew no one else would be around the office. It might work out after all.

The air felt fresh as he emerged from the building. The college was up on a hill above the yellow haze of the city. On the walk between the classroom and his office, Phil began to formulate his next novel: a successful novelist suffering a prolonged writer's block meets a flighty young poetess at a writers' conference. He felt better than he had in weeks, free to stretch without breaking delicate objects.

Phil greeted the department secretary, a grim, plump woman of fifty, with an unaccustomed smile. He was not one of her boys, never bought her flowers on Secretary Day or complimented her on the arrangement of velvet bows in her hair.

She did not return his smile. 'Bob was looking for you.'

Just then the chairman popped his head out of his office. 'Do you have some free time now, Phil?'

Something about the official air of the request disturbed Phil. He rarely talked to Bob Williams, a white-haired Harvard man, a real scholar, so everyone said, who looked New England but talked Kansas. A pleasant enough fellow, but someone you could only exchange greetings with.

Phil stared across the desk at the stern portrait of Jonathan Swift. Not one of his favorites.

'A rather serious situation has developed. You have a student in your writing class, Jane Wood?'

Phil nodded, shifted his body around in the narrow chair. The chairman's voice sounded as if from the stage of a hushed theater.

'She lodged a complaint against you.' Here Bob Williams paused, searching for some way to express the next statement. He grimaced, not really the right word to express the gravity of his thin dry mouth.

'She told me you had harassed her sexually.' The chairman looked at him, probably with the hope that he would deny the charge.

'Are you the only one she's talked to?'

'Yes I believe so, but I'm afraid she wants to bring the matter before the dean.'

'That's ridiculous. I've taught here for fifteen years.' If only he could explain what really happened but not to Bob Williams; someone else could see the nuances, someone else might laugh the girl away.

Williams unfolded his hands, his expression that of the sick room.'We'll back you as much as we can. You've always been popular with students.'

'Thank you,' Phil said contritely, like a gigantic schoolboy. 'But if she raises the issue before the whole college, I don't know.'

Phil wanted to say he hadn't touched her, not really. It was blackmail, some anger she had, the bitch. 'I didn't harass her.'

'Yes, of course.' The chairman produced a bleak smile. 'But it's her word against yours and your reputation. If she goes to the dean, the president, we'll have to have a hearing. Who knows how far it could go.' He paused.

'Christ! So what can I do?'

'Nothing at the moment till we know what she's going to do. But I wanted you to be aware of the situation.'

Bob asked after Phil's wife and they both mentioned vague invitations for dinner.

Phil left the office, his face moist, his clothes clinging to his body. He did not look at the secretary though he felt her glance, but walked silently by her shiny topknot of hair.

No one to talk to. Phil closed his office door. He pushed a pile of student papers from the center of his desk, rested his hands, then his elbows on the cool metal. He rubbed his eyes, then peered out the window at the city, not his town. He could leave without sadness.

A knock at the door. A small man in a wrinkled striped shirt entered before Phil could speak. Dave Javits calling round for their usual Friday afternoon drink. Poor Dave, a widower with fantasies about young women. For a moment Phil thought of pouring it all out; Dave might make a good joke of it.

'Not today. My wife's having some friends over. She wants me home early. You know what it's like,' Phil invented. Even Dave with his obvious sexual jokes would think Phil mad for grabbing a student. They had had long discussions on the art of manipulation, but it was not clear that Dave Javits had ever seduced anyone but his dead wife.

Dave mumbled something about a paper he was working on. An eighteenth-century man who hadn't published anything in twenty years, he was one of the small department's many mediocrities.

After he left, Phil felt paralysed. Finally he began to gather up his papers and books. When he reached his car he knew he could not go home, not without his wife seeing his distress. He began walking down into the city, a journey Phil hadn't taken in years.

Third Street. Even the name had no identity. Cars rolled up the wide avenue toward the distant bluish foothills of the Rockies. How disappointed Phil had been when he arrived fifteen years ago from New York to find the great mountains did not embrace the city. Denver existed quite apart from the Rockies, a sham of a city with no heart, no brain.

Phil wanted to burrow in some alleyway, away from the march of white towers, J.C. Penney's and Woolworth's. Young girls rushed by, running to catch buses, feet aching from a day behind the counter, fingers numb from the typewriter. Everyone leaving for the weekend, a soon-to-be-desert city. Phil realized he was walking against the tide and moved to the inner part of the sidewalk.

A thin girl with curly hair approached him. If it were Jane, what would he say, would he plead or shout at her? But it was not. He must not faint, for a middle-aged man who fainted was either ridiculous or very ill.

Phil pushed open the door of the Satire Lounge. Soothing darkness. He stumbled down the steps to the bar, blinking to rid himself of the bright dots.

Two old men watched him approach. One nodded to Phil, who, seeing the grizzled face of a drunk, turned away and sat at the other end of the bar.

'A Martini,' he called out to the bartender. A woman in a grey raincoat jiggled the pinball machine in the far corner of the large room and cursed.

He could leave, maybe survive by writing, just writing. Phil smiled at his fantasy, but it was possible even this late. His life, the quotidian, had become dull especially when looked at from the outside.

The woman at the pinball machine turned, but seemed afraid to leave off jiggling and slamming the machine. She had a desperate look about her pale, horsy face.

Phil ordered another Martini. Jane was pitiful and he a fool. No need to be angry, to make a scene. He would talk to her.

'Are you ready?' The drunk's question resounded throughout the room.

He walked over to Phil and grabbed his shoulder. 'Are you ready for today?' A shattering laugh. Phil pulled away and walked out of the bar.

Garbage swirled through the empty streets like tumbleweed. A plastic bag flew towards him and latched on to his leg. It was only when he came back to the college and his car that he realized he had walked all the way up there with the bag still clinging to him.

Phil laughed at the red lights as he drove home. When he turned into his driveway, he let the car travel almost to the door of the garage before he stepped on the brakes.

He walked in humming. But after his wife greeted him with a look of irritation because he was late, Phil felt despair again.

He sat unmoving at his accustomed place at the table while Carol called the two boys and then set the dishes down. His voice as he greeted his sons sounded like it came from someone else, a loud, peremptory voice sternly enquiring after school.

His wife had a manly look, her grey hair tied back in a short ponytail, her broad shoulders held straight as she dished out potatoes and beef stew. She might ask for a divorce. All these years Carol knew about his affairs, must know, but none were serious, not really, none threatened her position. Carol had kept her silence, so had he. If it all came out in the open?

Now she was clearing off the plates. The boys brought in the pie and his coffee. They finished quickly and raced off to the television room.

'You look tired,' Carol said. 'Have you talked to a lot of students today?' The irritation hadn't lasted long, it never did.

'Just the usual.' He felt no passion for this heavy woman, nothing like that for years, typical he supposed. They were friendly companions. He felt tears rising. She was the mother of his children.

What was she saying? What was she saying?

'You want to have Harriet and Sam for dinner next Friday? I was thinking it was about time.'

Phil brooded the whole weekend. His wife kept tactfully away, thinking probably it was one his moods between books. But he would have welcomed any conversation, if only to take his mind off his predicament.

He did not banter with his sons in the usual half-sarcastic, half-patronizing way, but they scarcely noticed. The older one was dating; the younger preferred to chase a Frisbee around the yard. What difference did he make to anyone? Phil sat on the patio, his face sour.

When he arrived at his office on Monday, Phil expected to see a note from the chairman, but his mailbox was empty. He waited all Monday and subsequent days for some sign, some event which would signal the beginning of his 'undoing' as he half-jokingly referred to it in his mind.

Then he fantasized about relief. Jane Wood left the school; she became very ill over the weekend, a horrible accident, a death in the family, for he expected no mercy from her. The crazy bitch, she would never relent.

Phil stopped himself from knocking on the chairman's door to ask if anything had happened. He did not want to appear desperate; then it would all be over for him.

Phil told Julie he could not see her that week; he did not want to risk himself further. And Julie seemed so young, her soft face lacking not intelligence but the awareness which comes with age and sexual experience. He would be seducing a child.

On Friday afternoon after his class, Phil was sorting through some student stories when Jane Wood slipped into his office. Phil had to swallow before he could talk, managing only a wry 'Hello, where have you been?' She was still his student, a student who had disappeared from class for two weeks now. He had a right to ask.

She pushed a pink slip of paper across the desk. 'You don't have to worry, I'm dropping your course. You have to sign because it's so late into the term.' She explained her presence in his office.

Without a word Phil signed the wrinkled paper. Probably she had clutched it all the way from the registrar to his office. Her pass to freedom, his reprieve. His signature was a scrawl.

Jane pushed the slip into her pocket, stood up and adjusted her knapsack on her back. Dressed like a boy in straight jeans and a plaid shirt, she was rather appealing. Phil surveyed her body with an amused expression.

Jane followed his glance. 'I read one of your novels this weekend.'

'Could you find a copy? I'm surprised.' The old joke about literary failure. Phil grinned at her. Perhaps the thing need not end on a bad note.

She kept a straight face.

'I thought I'd find out more about you, but it wasn't you.' Phil didn't know what to say to this.

'I mean you couldn't have had those affairs and left your wife. It's all fantasy isn't it and you're a coward.' It was the first time he had seen her smile, not a smile really. Though his hand shook with rage, he wanted to touch her mouth.

'Get out of here!'

Jane fumbled with her knapsack, pulled out a black and shiny object. It was a gun she was pointing at him almost nonchalantly.

'How ridiculous.' Phil made an effort to keep his voice low and calm. It could not be real.

'How does it feel?'

He wanted to say 'You're mad' but the words didn't emerge though he felt his lips move.

'Do you know anything, do you feel anything? Tell me, tell me.'

She came towards him silently now, holding the gun like a live animal, the smile gone from her face.

'You give that to me.' His chin and lower lip were twitching. His flesh, his body always so solid, so firm around him, grew soft. He could not have moved. She wanted to give him something, he understood now, the gun was her present; she wanted him to have its eruption.

'Please give me...' His voice had gone high.

'Here,' she whispered, lifting the gun, pointing it at his face. She squeezed the trigger.

A spray of icy water struck his forehead. Phil struggled to see through a stream of water, sweat and tears. They were tears he had not experienced since childhood, tears of rage as if some precious toy had been torn from him, mocked and destroyed. Yet till that moment he had not known it was precious.

Phil began wiping his face, first with his hand and then with a handkerchief which he remembered was in his pocket. There was a knock at the open door. Jane turned and darted out past Dave Javits.

'What was that all about? She looked pretty upset.'

'Oh nothing.' Phil was trembling, was hoping he wouldn't be sick.

'Not one of your heartbreaks?' Dave winked.

'Yeah.' Phil marvelled at the cool sound of his voice. 'That's it, if you really want to know.'

I see a long coat wide open, teeny shorts and high bare legs. She walks around the horseshoe counter till she sits down across from me. How could you not notice this giantess, lean as a sapling with the pale skin and creased eyes of a night bird? The waiter knows her, so do a couple of the bus drivers and the men who roll beer kegs into the bars on Colfax. But I don't cotton on to her. Because I'm doodling in my soothsayer's pad, thinking that if I had powers I'd wish myself away from here.

I'm having my coffee at White Spot early in the morning before my stint at the old age home. I cook for the ladies the good food I miss: thick bacon and cornbread so silky you could wear it. I ask, 'What does this remind you of?' If they shake their head, I turn up their hands, trace the longest line and say, 'You have not lived long enough to know.' Sometimes I bring a record to the home, maybe Bessie Smith or someone singing, 'You made me love you.' I like to liven the old ladies even if they say 'Who's that?' and upset their trays.

My real job is telling people who they'll be. I'm an astrologer. If I have to, I'll read palms though I don't like all those broken lines. Tomas says to me, 'For a down home girl you sure up in the clouds.' He's Columbian, a short chunky saxophone player with long black hair and a beard to match. With my flaxen hair, we look like the princess and the goblin together. Only I'm not a pretty lady. My face is too long for that, but Tomas tells me how soft and shapely my breasts are. We can make love for hours once we get going.

Next time I see my giantess I'm not even surprised. After you notice someone in Denver you keep meeting them. They're like floaters in your eye, appearing disappearing, moving around but always there. It's that kind of city where despite the thousands there are only the people you're destined to know.

She's in Emily's Bead Shop picking out alphabet beads, the kind you see on newborn baby bracelets. I'm putting up my cards here and across the street at the One Hand Bookstore where people in this bland city of cowpokes have other worldly needs.

She watches me pin up my trademark, a moon face like the one I showed my little sisters after mom died: 'That's her looking after you.' But I was scared of her sooty mouth.

'I could use a reading,' she says coming up behind me. When I turn to look at her, I don't just recognize her from White Spot. There's some time before that, some time I can't remember I was knowing her.

Usually I do my readings at White Spot but when Cindy asks me to come to her place, I agree because she's such a different one. I tell myself I need to know more about her. Not just that I'm a nosey parker. What people don't understand about charts is that we look at the person and shape our readings around what we see. And I'm not talking about auras. There's nothing I can do about the minute of your birth, but how you've lived, there's my coloring and shading.

I find Cindy's house just off Colfax, a shambling clapboard place, yellow fading and garbage in the front yard. I'm thinking she could be a danger but I'm a foolhardy girl. It's how I got together with Tomas who caught me sauntering around the Mission in San Francisco. She opens the door to her one room. Bed in the corner, kitchenette but no smell of cooking. An all together room, hard and cold as if no life was ever lived there.

We sit at the square white table. I take out her chart and begin my explanation but she seems not interested as if she heard this all before. I'm speaking to her white profile. I talk about her moon in Scorpio, her ascendant in Libra. I point to a trine which shows why her life won't settle, but she says nothing.

She puts her finger on her name which I'd written in silver pen across the top. 'What d'you write that for?'

'I always do. Why not?' It's like naming a child.

She shows me her profile again.

'I'll cross it out if it bothers you.' I take out my pen.

'Just leave it. Cindy's not my name. Not my real name. That's all.'

'But we should have your real name.' I think of these charts as alive, their truths weaving around the circles like moons. 'Really. It would be better for you.'

'You're joking.'

I shake my head.

'Okay. Make it Elena.'

'That's pretty,' I say and she raises her eyebrows.

She gives me only her first name. Maybe she doesn't believe in last names just as she doesn't care about her own story sketched out for her in all its tragedy. Yet I had not put it so.

When I cross out 'Cindy' and write 'Elena', the chart seems to shiver as if to shake off a lie.

She grabs my hand and at first I'm afraid she's turned because there's something ice hot about her. But she places her own hand palm up in mine.

'I'm so afraid,' she says.

'You want a palm reading too?'

I look at the long white hand. Maybe the sudden flash of light from the window blinds me, for at first I see no lines, as if she were a wax woman. But then my eyes sharpen and I think what to tell her. 'What would you like to know?'

'Everything,' she says.

I look and then turn away from the waxen palm resting in my hand. It's why I could not see lines at first because hers are so broken, heart and life. Fine breaks as if she had many lives.

I say, 'You've had lots of changes.'

She nods.

'And these changes will continue.' I sound like one of those crystal ball women with a shawl over my head.

'But will I live?'

It seems looking at her palm that she should have died long ago. I turn my other hand over to look at my lifeline and see for the first time, a break, minute but there.

'You mean how long you'll live? I can't say. Nobody can.'

'He did. He said I would die this year.'

51

I look down at her palm and then at her serious face. 'You know how impossible it would be to say that.'

'But he knew.'

'He knew how to scare you silly. Who is this guy?'

She gives me a little smile. 'Just a guy I know.'

I give her hand a squeeze. 'You will live for so long you will be bored with living.'

I don't charge for the palm reading. Why when I never said the truth.

She says, 'Can you read me again sometime?'

'You mean your palm? But nothing changes except real slow.'

'I don't care. I just want to hear you read me. I'll pay.'

I wish she didn't have my phone number. There's something about her pale brittle face I don't want to get involved in. But I agree.

When I reach home Tomas is lying on the sofa with his sax clasped to his chest. His eyes are shut and the room smells of dope. I sit on the sofa and stroke his soft black hair.

'You should've waited for me,' I say.

'There's another one there.' He points to a fat little joint sitting on our crate of a living room table.

But I don't want to smoke. Lately it's made the world tremble and crack. I have to shut my eyes to keep the edges from cutting into me.

I drop off my bag in the bedroom. The bed looks beaten up as if he's been tousling with his dreams. We live in different time zones. He comes in from his gig at 3am while I'm sleeping, and I wake and leave for my morning with the old ladies before he comes to.

'Paula,' he calls out.

I come back to the living room. He smooths and resmooths his moustache and beard. 'Paula I can't do it anymore.'

If only he would rise up, I could make him fried eggs and potatoes. I could do for him, but he's got his sad goblin look.

'Their music is shit. I play and they say no you must not go there. So last night I leave.'

Tomas is the star of the group, who they come for but he doesn't want to play the tuneful tunes, the jazz numbers people can dance to. He's made his own music.

It happened before in San Francisco when he'd gone off on a tangent night after night till the group told him they could not play with him anymore. And they were friends, fellow Columbians. When he came to Denver for a gig where he could earn real money, he said, I will forget myself.

He says his saxophone is possessed so what can he do? Every time he puts his lips on it a spirit rushes through the twisted brass and surges into him. 'It plays me,' he says.

'And you tell me I'm a spooky girl.' He's refused to tell me his time of birth. He doesn't want to be read by the priestess of Denver he says shaking a finger, his big long-haired head to one side. I love him when he looks at me like that as if I am his wayward woman. 'I have all you are,' he whispers when we make love.

'Just go back tonight,' I say. 'I'll come with you.'

'I don't want you see me playing shit.'

He strokes my cheek. 'Okay. I go back. I say sorry.' Slowly he rises with the saxophone still in his arms and wanders into the bedroom. I know to leave him there till nightfall.

Elena asks for another reading. I tell her it'll be the same, but she pleads. We're sitting side by side at the counter of White Spot when she flourishes her hand. Something about the dimness of the day makes her palm clearer to me.

'So tell me will I die this year?' She grins. I have given her real optimism. I see many deaths and something rises from her palm. I ask her to curl her hand and I see a child born.

'You got it wrong. I had two.' She holds up her long narrow fingers. 'Two girls.' She looks at me with hard eyes. Then she laughs and I laugh with her but don't understand why.

'I was just a kid. I was so young. So they took them away. Lisette and Michelle.'

53

'Pretty names,' I say. I was hoping she would say I've an-other life much better than the one you've seen in which my girls dance around me.

She puts a ten-dollar bill in my hand. I feel I shouldn't ac-cept because I've lied again, but if I don't she'll wonder about this and think about the mistake I've made about her children, and then she'll begin to doubt.

I think Tomas has settled in with the group until one evening he says, 'I can't do this.'

I say anything, that we'll return to San Francisco. If only he plays just a few more months here, then we'll find something else back there. Maybe persuade his friends to take him on again. He shakes his head and tells me his good friend Luis in San Francisco, a Columbian boy, talks about going back home. Suddenly I feel us lost as if we missed the towers of Denver and landed on our asses in the great plain which stretches east.

I make him the dinner he likes with beans and rice and then I tell him I'm going with him tonight to keep him from wander-ing. 'I'll be your lady.' He holds me then puts his big sad head against my breasts.

I sit with the other girlfriends at a table near the front while the guys play notes to each other. The drummer, a lean black guy with a sweet smile and low-slung eyelids, sits there smok-ing. I'm watching Tomas in a motherly way hoping he'll mix with the others, but he's blowing whispers into his sax.

I'm with a glum bunch. The drummer's girlfriend has may-be lost her words: she's skinny as anything with white blonde hair bleached to singe. There's Norma who is older than us and works as a secretary. She's the trumpet player's weekday woman.

The set starts mellow till Tomas steps out from the group for his solo, his face raised to the light. He walks into the tables still playing, eyes shut as if the others don't exist. I want to grab him but he doesn't stand still. The sounds go on and on; they grow more broken, not even music any more. I look back at the group. The trumpet player says 'C'mon man.' I try to make

Tomas look at me, but his eyes are half closed. 'Don't leave,' I whisper.

The people at the tables turn back to their drinks, their talk. She's still listening, a woman at the next table, the only one apart from me who can bear to hear those sounds like a woman crying her heart out.

The bass player takes up the thread of something Tomas's playing, maybe just a note. And then the trumpet player pushes in. Tomas's eyes open at the intrusion and he lowers the sax and wanders back to them.

Nobody claps for Tomas's solo except me and the woman at the next table. Then she stands up and goes off to the ladies room, is in there a long time, long enough for the guys to finish the set and for Tomas to come to me.

'You shouldn't do that,' I say. 'They won't want you.'

'I am who they want.'

'But they won't keep wanting.'

She comes back and I see Elena, Elena with blonde hair. She comes over to us, her face sleepy behind the sharp black circling her eyes, her dead white skin.

She ignores me like the women do at these gigs. She says to Tomas, 'You were playing for me weren't you?' Taps him on the shoulder.

She sounds dopey, and I know what she was doing in the bathroom so long.

He gives her one of his smiles. 'Sure.'

She struggles through the tables.

He's been playing with his empty glass, turning it round and round. 'Lost lady,' he says.

'You said that last time,' Elena says. We're sitting at the square white table in the square white room flooded with winter sun. It's so cold I'm imagining we're inside an ice cube.

'I told you the lines don't change.' I don't like the way she looks. Partly it's the weird turban she's wearing as if she's the palm reader.

She gives me one of her looks. I remember from junior high, the tough girls with their straightened hair and Cleopatra eyes.

I try to shrug. 'Don't you believe in heat?'

'I don't control it.'

'Well I'm a Tennessee girl so this is more than I can take.' I get up to leave. I don't even want her money.

She grabs my arm and holds it so tightly that if I tried to get away we might even be fighting. 'Tell me. You're not telling me. I can see the broken lines.'

I sit back down and she lets go of me. I take her palm and trace a couple of lines. 'Maybe they are.'

'So?'

'So you might get sick.'

She pulls away. 'You're not telling me. All this time I'm a dead woman and you're not telling me.'

I shake my head. Then I say, 'I don't believe in palms. Not really. They're just lines you're born with. What does that mean?'

'So it's true then?'

'I don't know and neither does anyone.'

She's crying but not like a normal person who tries to hold back or puts their hands over their eyes. No she's crying as if her face were a stone miraculously producing tears.

She says, 'Go.'

'You're going to be okay,' I say.

'Just go.'

When the call comes in the middle of the night, Tomas is still not back. I'm shaking as I pick up the phone, thinking of him lying in the street. But I hear someone struggling to catch their breath.

'Who is this?' I ask. Then I hang up the phone fast.

It rings again and I bury myself beneath pillows. I hate phantom phone calls. It doesn't stop ringing and by now my heart's crazy dancing.

I pick up the phone and before I can speak, she says, 'It's me Elena. I had to hear you. I'm so fucked.'

'Jesus body. You scared me.'

'I'm feeling like maybe my life could end. Right now it would end. Or I would end it so I wouldn't have to be afraid.'

I think of her palm stretched out beside her body.

'He's after me. Cause I owe him. He says if I don't pay.'

So it's money she wants. I'm calmer now. I say, 'Look I'm sorry but...'

'I'm not asking you for anything. Not for anything.'

'Okay,' I say, 'maybe it's not so bad as you think. Maybe he just wants to scare you.' I think of her face so pretty when she smiles and then like a white mask clowns wear.

'I wanted to hear you.'

After that I turn lights on all over the flat and make myself a mu tea. I tell myself she is wiser than me. I put on Dionne singing 'You'll never get to heaven if you break my heart.' I love her sweet voice and how she lifts the words even the sad ones. Soon Tomas will be home and I will curl around him, my hairy dark man like a sturdy tree in the barrens of Denver.

I keep expecting another night call from her. Sometimes I even lay awake waiting for someone to bad-mouth their way through the phone to me. I'm draggy with my old ladies, but do they notice? Do they even remember me one day to the next?

I go to White Spot, Emily's Bead Shop, but never do I see her. One day I'm walking up Colfax bound for the nursing home when she comes towards me, grand in her long purple coat flaring open to a silky black skirt. First I think she's with someone, a lanky guy with a mane of red hair. The guy disappears as she approaches me so I'm not sure if I saw his hand on her. Her face is triumphant as she walks. I'm thinking she won't even acknowledge me, doesn't even seem to see me, until we're nearly passing each other and she taps my shoulder.

'You,' she says.

I ask how she is there in the middle of this godforsaken street of hard men and cowboys, drunks and paupers.

'I'm good. Because of you. I told myself I can outlive my death. Who cares what he says.' She looks around as if searching for that guy, then holds up her palms.

'But what about the man who threatened you?'

'I just did what I had to do, didn't I?' she says and I understand that I shouldn't ask about him again.

When I reach my old ladies, they tell me that Betty has died. She's my cranky lady who will eat my cornbread and then say 'No, not right.' We are both Tennessee girls and she can sing all the old country numbers. She was one of the sturdy ones so I'm shaken more than I want to be.

I'm flipping the pages of the *Denver Post*. I usually don't buy it but one of my ladies wanted me to read the news to her. What she really missed was the smell of the paper. She cared nothing for what the black print said.

Tomas lies on the sofa. He's not working his gig anymore.

'Maybe we should go back,' I say.

He doesn't say anything.

'You could maybe get back together with Carlos and the others. At least we'd be away from here.'

Still he doesn't say anything. He hasn't played for days.

'What do you think?'

Then he tells me they're leaving, all the Columbians he played with. 'They want home. They want have their feet on the ground.'

I take his hand and look at the palm. I've never read him but I know the lines are deep and strong. I trace them with my finger. They are like furrows cut into him and they will lead him away from me.

'Paula, Paula.' He takes his hand away and puts his arms around me. I have been his house. Then he says how he needs to sleep. It's all he does every day, wakes to sleep.

He walks into the bedroom with the halting movement of an old man.

I'm back to my paper again, the pages like the swishing of a crinoline. Me as one of the twelve dancing princesses in fourth grade, pink crepe paper hanging from the stiff shelves of veil.

There's a story about a woman attacked in Capitol Hill early one morning. They don't say her name but she was stabbed over on 17th near where Elena lives.

Two days pass and the paper says they found the attacker, someone the woman knew. I think of the guy who predicted Elena's death. I try to remember the red-haired man who slipped away when I saw her on Colfax, but all I see is his narrow face as if he had only a profile. I made her not afraid and now he's finally caught up with her. Even if I wanted to I couldn't phone her to see if she's okay. I don't have a number. There's no reason to call now that she knows what her palm says and is not afraid. No reason.

I'm back in front of the yellow clapboard shack of a house which looks like it should sit at the end of a dirt road in some wrong side of the tracks deepest Appalachia. I have no problem getting in because the front door lock is broken. I climb and reach the door which rings hollow with my knock. I'm hoping she's out because what will I say? That I thought she was possibly a murdered woman?

A woman with long black hair opens the door. Behind her in the white room with the white table, a man sits on the bed with his shirt open. The place smells of sex and his smoking. She's looks blank when I ask for Elena. Then I say 'Cindy' and she says, 'Oh her. She doesn't use this place anymore.'

I look from her to the man and think what a fool I've been. She doesn't know where she actually lives.

'But she's somewhere in Denver, isn't she.'

'Who are you?'

'I'm just. I'm just her palm reader.'

She shuts the door on me.

Next day the paper has more details about the victim but no picture. Elena in her turban sauntering, not thinking for once that her palm lines could tangle her. 'There's no destiny,' Tomas once said. 'We're just blind men.'

59

Then the story disappears from the newspaper. I think of Elena as a lucky charm I found and lost. Because I took my mind off her she will no longer appear to me.

We've given notice and have weeks to go before we return to San Francisco. Tomas doesn't say but I know what going back means to him though he promises to try again. Who's he going to try with now that his buddies have left?

I'm saying goodbye to my old ladies slowly, each day I repeat so that maybe when I actually disappear from their lives they will remember that I was here and then I left. When I leave them I walk through the park, my usual diversion before heading home. I have to stop myself rushing back, calling 'Tomas' as if he might not be there. I walk around and around till I have talked to myself enough for calm.

It's not a normal park where kids play and old people sit contemplating. Two children of god, white-faced teens, approach me with an offer of bed and prayer and when I shake my head whisper a blessing. An old man offers me a tract. When I refuse, I hear him damn me to hell. Once I saw a soldier calmly throwing away the contents of his suitcase.

Then through the budding trees I see a tall woman walking slowly, her head in a turban, a man with a camera following her, a group standing beyond him.

I follow them as they follow her. She turns and kneels before a tree. She moves on, approaches a man, the only other actor in this silent film. She puts her hands in prayer in front of him but he shakes his head. She continues her stroll, her narrow head held up.

I discover that they are film students making a movie. They saw Elena on Colfax tall as anything in her turban and just knew she was the one to play the odd one.

'But she's not,' I want to say.

They're calling it 'Who are we when we are not?' I move closer. I just want to make sure that she is she and not some thin cloud between the trees and that all the deaths I saw in her palm have eluded her.

The guy with the camera touches my arm to stop me. 'We got her just right now,' he whispers. 'She won't repeat anything. Says it's bad luck.'

She moves with deliberate long steps like some slow motion giraffe on the savannah. I kiss my palm and then raise it. My palm to hers. She never sees me but I give back her destiny.

Natalie roams the hallway. She and Lucky are janitors of a white stucco apartment building, two stories which shake when the big trucks go by and a basement with vinyl floors where they live. She vacuums the thin beige carpet in the front hall. She's waiting for doors to open.

She pauses outside Sally's apartment. The doors are so flimsy she can hear conversations without even trying. Sally's around during the day in her kimono, her face glazed with makeup for her evening selling tickets at Greyhound. But there's a stillness on the other side of Sally's door as if she hasn't emerged from her satin sheets.

Natalie climbs to the second floor to collect the late rent from Annie, not that she has to, not that it is so late. But she wants to talk to someone for Lucky has been away since yesterday morning, and he never calls. 'It's not me,' he says of his voice over the telephone as if he needs all of himself to be there when he speaks to her. Even if he is gone just for the day, when he returns he picks her up and whirls her around, she a long-limbed girlish woman with a narrow face and dark downturned eyes. 'Worry eyes,' Lucky calls them.

She knocks softly so as not to wake Annie's next door neighbor, Mr Henry, a man with a face of pitted stone and two braids up the back of his head. He sleeps all day beneath windows shrouded with blankets and works nights in a factory.

Lucky calls her Annie Oakley because when she came round to see the apartment she wore cowboy boots and a fringed leather jacket. Annie with her shiny black hair and one feather earring. She waitresses at night but during the day sits in the sunlight of her little bedroom twisting wire around silver beads and turquoise stones.

Once when they shared a pipe filled with grass, Annie started dancing by herself. She beckoned to Natalie.

'I can't,' Natalie said, pointing to her legs, 'they don't dance.'

But around and around they went, Annie holding her like a cowboy when she stumbled. They smoked some more and she put on Ravi Shankar. When Natalie woke they were lying side by side in the darkness their hands clasped.

As she begins to turn away, the door opens. No Annie but a tall lean guy with a flaming bush of hair.

'She's gone to mountains,' he says. Natalie feels unnerved by his watchful eyes, the way he pulls at his beard.

'Tell her she's overdue with the rent.' She had not meant to sound like that. Annie was always late but she paid in the end.

He stares at her still with the door half closed. 'Yeah I'll tell.'

What does she really know about Annie? The tenants come and go. They bring their friends but Natalie says nothing unless there's trouble. She hasn't spoken to Mr Henry for months. He pays his rent while she sleeps, slipping a check under her door. Once she saw him in the street; he looked hunched over in his wide coat, hurrying along as if afraid of the day.

She returns to her flat because no one is around. Later there'll be Sally, and then Natalie will drive to the college. Each course she takes is painful as if she has to swallow all the words she reads. That's the way to better yourself, she told Lucky.

He pointed to the Jesus he'd hung in the living room. He floats in a sky of sapphire and pink. Just his head with long blond hair, a full soft beard and a mouth beginning to smile. He is the way, Lucky said, truly the only way for Jesus had lifted Lucky from the flames licking his heels and brought him to her.

When they first moved to Denver she tried Lucky with courses at the community college. She imagined him a college boy, his books under his muscular arms, but Lucky squirmed in the classes. What he wanted was to drive a truck, so badly he wanted it that she had to say yes, Lucky with his smile that won her over when she was not looking to be won. And then dragged her all the way from Chicago to Denver and into the sunshine. She would still be home with her parents, asleep on the brocaded brown sofa, the television mumbling in the curtained room.

'You were buried,' Lucky said.

'I was just tired.' The doctor said some kind of virus made her legs give way, but Lucky called it, 'God weariness.'

She thinks of him now high up in the cabin of the truck, turning the wheel on the bright highway. Then she draws the curtains so no one can see her from the street and reads her novel for English class about the gypsy boy running with the wilful girl across moors till they fall together into the land. She shuts her eyes, stretches out on the sofa with the book spread across her belly. Beneath her the rough material of the sofa becomes the coarse grass of the moors, her half shut eyes like the lowering sky, and the boy with his smell of earth presses deep within her.

'He came through the window,' Sally says. Natalie sits in the kitchen identical to her own, windowless with a row of brown plastic cabinets, but Sally has red checked mats and mugs with pictures of pert black cats while the real one, a dirty calico named Thomson after Sally's first husband, lies across the kitchen floor licking his broad white belly. Natalie never said a word about him though the lease says no pets. He has a disconcerting way of stopping suddenly, staring around with his tongue peeping through his mouth. Natalie thinks he's no cat but Sally's husband come back to glare at her.

'You don't mind my face?' Sally asked when Natalie knocked. Her door had been ajar which meant she was brewing a pot and open for anyone to join her. She's kept her white night cream on till it's time to make up for Greyhound. Sally knows every route out of Denver even the little stops on the slow buses. 'I say them for going to sleep.'

She talks about some woman who was attacked over on Seventeenth Street. 'You just have to wonder when you're safe.'

Natalie doesn't say anything. She dips her fork into her pie. She thinks of telling her about the man in Annie's flat. But Natalie decides that Sally should not know about Annie's personal life.

That night after she turns off all but the halo of lights around Jesus, she is so deep in her dreams, so buried there in the windowless bedroom below everyone that she does not hear Lucky come in. Above her Sally returns from Greyhound, the routes out of Denver running like rivulets of tears down her makeup, and Mr Henry climbs through the churning factory. And above them all, the flame-haired man walks back and forth pulling at the points of his beard. Natalie dreams of a woman who is just ahead of her, always just ahead.

Lucky's smell wakes her for he goes to her before he showers so she can hold his days away, the tang of his sweat, the dust from the road settled in his hair.

In the morning she tells him about the man in Annie's flat.

'So she's got a boyfriend finally. I thought she didn't like men,' he says.

'How do you know she didn't have one before?' She pulls his hair.

'Hey. I was just saying.' Lucky grins at her, tilting his head. They should have another go before he has to leave.

Natalie puts her hand on his chest. 'You don't think something weird happened? You should see him. He looks like a fox.'

'Maybe he's eaten her? If you're so worried tell him it's Annie's flat. He's gotta leave. You know what to do. I'm just your handy man.'

This time Lucky will be gone for a week up in Wyoming. 'Why don't you go out more?' he says.

But she trembles when she opens the door of the building into the sunlight and walks down the broad sidewalk beneath the gaze of the apartment blocks, the capitol building with its gold dome like a huge clown laughing at her.

After Lucky leaves she climbs to the second floor, her long thin legs heavy all of a sudden. The flame-haired man appears again at the door as soon as she knocks almost as if he is waiting for her. He leans on the doorway one hand grasping the knob of the door. He says that Annie's still up the mountain. And no he doesn't know when she'll be back.

Natalie can see only a corner of the room behind him, the edge of a maroon sofa, because he holds the door half closed.

There is a shadow over his eyes so that he can see her and maybe know what she wonders but she cannot read his face. She wants to say who are you but something happens to her legs. She stumbles towards him, tries to catch herself but already he puts his hand out to stop her falling and then he moves his hand up her bare arm. When he turns away, she sees how his red hair flows down the back of his neck, how his arms are flecked with red hairs.

She shuts her eyes and tries to bring back Annie, her cropped hair, the feather edged in blue, her bright eyes looking over Natalie as if to say come with me if you dare. Back in the flat she pulls down the blinds and begins taking slow steps till she is almost dancing. She takes off her clothes and moves faster till Jesus shakes below his halo and in the mirror she can see two of herself.

The next day she begins washing the front windows on the first floor. She climbs up to the second floor with the rag still in her hand as an excuse. She starts to walk down the hallway, then pauses outside Annie's door. She hears nothing or almost nothing. There is a step on the other side, and she moves away fast imagining him looking through the keyhole at her.

When Lucky returns she does not tell him that she has been back to Annie's flat. If he finds out that the red-haired man put his hand on Natalie, even just to steady her, he'll get a look in his eyes. Like she is some jewel which the slightest touch could tarnish.

He is full of talk of the truck and how with the money he's making they can move out to the mountains someday.

Natalie says, 'But I'm a city girl.'

'You'd get high on mountains.'

She imagines a lone house with no one to speak to but the bluish peaks she can barely see from Denver. 'I would die up there.'

He pays no mind to this. He's only back for one night. When he leaves in the morning, Natalie realizes she has been worrying all the time that he might ask about the man in Annie's flat, and she could never lie.

Natalie reads about the wilful girl marrying the milky-faced man she scorns and now she can no longer run over the dark hills, now she will die of him. She shuts the novel and suddenly wonders why she has never seen the flame-haired guy outside the apartment.

Natalie stares at Jesus, his narrow face covered in beard and framed by his long blond hair gleams in the dim light of the room. If only she says to herself, if only what? She sees his face, then his head and neck, his shoulders emerging, then all of him as he forces his way through the picture to be with her. She drags the curtains apart and as the light of the blue day falls on him Jesus goes back inside his halo.

'Not now glory girl,' Sally says as she stands in the doorway. That's Sally's nickname for her. She made up names for everyone in the building but Lucky who she said had given himself his name. Mr Henry is 'the creature' because she hears him pacing above her. 'We have one name and then another,' she says.

Her face without makeup or cold cream startles Natalie, as if Sally has been veiled all this time, and now she looks young and soft. 'I called in sick,' she says. Maybe this is one of the days when she is too much in the dark to come out.

Natalie looks out the big window at the top of the stairs. On the street a man walks by whistling. She thinks of the steps she must take to her car, on the glaring white sidewalk beneath the hot sky. Once she went out without her keys, drove all the way to the supermarket and back, and then discovered as she stood in the doorway with her bags that there was no way in. She had to ring Sally and put her food in her refrigerator till Lucky came home. Since then she keeps her keys in her back pocket of her jeans and touches them every so often.

She wills herself not to go back to Annie's flat. She could put a note under the door, the first warning for a tenant behind in their rent. But it is too soon. Lucky will wonder why she had not given Annie a full month. And if she does put a note under the door and nothing happens, then what?

She wanders back to her flat, carefully drawing the curtains because she does not like the window bare to the street when Lucky is not there. In the semi-darkness Jesus stares at her, his full pink mouth with just a hint of a smile. 'Go,' he says, 'go to him.'

She stands in front of Annie's door waiting. When it opens she will know what to say. She will say, 'You cannot live here anymore.' But when she knocks, the door opens fast and he is there so quickly, Natalie forgets what she prepared. The words come out: 'Where is she?'

Suddenly he pulls her in. She hears the door shut and she is against the wall, his body pressed on every part of her, his mouth on her mouth, his tongue like a snake inside her. And his smell all around her of damp and loamy woods. Then he steps back, his hands in the air as if surrendering.

She is out of the flat and running down the hallway. That night she dreams of Annie or someone who was Annie beckoning to her from inside a tall room. Down there in the dark of a Denver night, alone in the wide bed with Lucky rolling down the highway, she feels herself rise, then she is flying through the building, no longer gawky, her legs trailing beyond her like the tail of a comet. She flies above the heads of the sleepers and he flies with her, the man with the red mane.

'They found him,' Sally says when Natalie sits down at the wooden table. 'He was someone she met in a bar who followed her. It's the way. It always is. You have to be careful who you let into your life. But then you have Lucky who's such a cutie.' Sally went out with men she met over the ticket counter and sometimes they lasted more than a month. 'I want to get married, not be married,' Sally always said.

The next day Natalie decides to stay in her flat. She fears that somehow she will find herself up on the second floor again, somehow she will not be able to control her legs and Annie's door will open.

Lucky is not home for another three days. When she pulls the curtains she sees a day rare in Denver when the blaring sunlight is hidden by a downpour which will go on and on, a cloak of rain. Suddenly she is dressing and pulling out a great old umbrella from when she lived in Chicago and there was real rain.

As Natalie walks the darkened streets, everything is muted, even the gold dome, and the foothills have disappeared in the greyness. Up on Colfax, she stops to have coffee in White Spot. We don't belong except in the rain, she thinks of the bedraggled group sitting around the counter, their backs hunched against the sky. The large front windows of the restaurant are clouded with their breath, and in the stain of humidity she sees a long face take shape and then disappear.

Two days go by and Natalie has not gone up there. She can still smell the flame-haired man though she has showered several times since he pressed himself on her. Soon the month will be over and she will have no rent for number twenty-five and the landlord will ask. Lucky will wonder why she cannot do it, she who always collects the late rents because he is too soft.

She climbs the stairs with her vacuum cleaner, pulling it along slowly till she is almost at Annie's door. She stops and holds herself close because the door is ajar. She shudders, walks away fast and waits at the end of the hallway but there is no movement. Finally she walks back and stands before it. Her knock makes the wooden door move slightly so that she can see a sliver of room. No one comes and there's a stillness in there she hasn't known before.

Natalie knocks louder. She knows she should not do this alone, but she pushes the door and calls out 'Hello.' She waits with her hand on her neck. Then she walks into the sunlit living room. There's a maroon sofa just like hers, everything just like her rooms except no Jesus with his halo. There is no one but she sees the door to the bedroom is shut. She hears murmuring from the room like someone talking in their sleep. She steps closer but still cannot make out any words. She whispers 'Is anyone there?' The murmuring doesn't stop as if it comes from inside her like a heightened breathing.

She stands beside the bedroom door. She imagines Annie laughing at her. 'Why not?' Annie says.

'Because I don't want.'

'Don't want what?'

'No,' she whispers, 'no, I cannot,' and is ready to flee.

'But you do,' Annie says. And now Natalie smells damp and loamy woods.

And then she pushes the door.

'Go down to that point of light, down through your self.'

Pushing her way through dark waters, hands moving like a dying crab.

'Now light grows, streams of gold light rush down your arms.'

Wave upon wave upon blind eyes and curled hands, while all others burnish from the light.

'Come back now.'

The sun moving up her legs, belly, throat, her clenched eyes. The blurred teacher with head bowed, legs crossed, fingers touching fingers, the long room windowing the city.

'I felt so close that time, as if I were seeing my real self, without fear. I'm usually so afraid of what I might see,' Moira said, pulling a purple halter-top over her breasts.

Alice drew her shirt over her leotard; she did not like to undress in the locker-room common to all. Again Moira's smell, her damp skin, the curled hairs when she lifted her arms to bring down her knapsack. Moira had asked her first and then they had gone to lunch several times and to the art museum.

'Sunday afternoon and you know where I live,' Alice said. Moira was apt to forget with so many men drifting in her life. Alice went down the stairs, her steps small and quick, her head leaning to one side.

He stood there on the other side of the street. Alice looked and looked the other way. He was too young, his face a pale oval, his wasted body leaning on silver crutches. His eyes were on her that she knew as they both waited for cars to pass, her body warm and elastic from yoga, now growing taut. Finally a car stopped, the driver beckoning for him to cross. He did not move, his face reddening as he watched her. Alice waited, then began to cross.

On the opposite curb she heard him whisper softly, so softly that had she been walking a foot away she would not have heard him. 'Fuck you.' A whisper. She kept walking now faster, but the words brushed against her so soft and yet a curse, an endearment, yes an endearment.

Alice kneeled and crossed herself in the long dark nave. She lit a blue candle and stood before it, eyes shut, mouth tasting of wine, mumbling to God of her mother, of Moira, of the man braced against silver crutches.

She shielded her eyes from the sunlight. On the steps a small crowd gathered around a white-robed priest. A baby was offered to him. When he removed his gold hat, his white hair shone. She crossed the street to go to the Salvation Army thrift shop. Next to it in the doorway of a pinball alley, a man asked if she wanted a ride: 'I can take you where you want to go'.

There must be rhythm, an order to all this. Alice held up a length of yellow lace as she looked out at the street. She heard the persistence of the church bells, ringing to her. She turned back to the store. Rows of white men's shirts moving in the breeze from the open door, silky nightgowns and prom dresses marked by many hands. They waited to be worn again. Alice wanted not to feel sad, to be pitched down.

She stopped to speak with the old man who sold newspapers from the narrow passage of his shop. He was lonely and could not stop talking, his thin mouth moving quickly over the words. 'A girl was raped.' His tongue darted out of his mouth. 'He climbed through the window, over on Seventeenth Street.'

She tucked the newspaper under her arm and continued up the street to her apartment. Her neighborhood, the girl waking in the night to be possessed, to become another.

The sun had moved over the wooden floor. Alice had to shake herself from watching dust particles descend in the broad beam of light. Her cats roamed about her feet. She shut her eyes for a moment and when she opened them noticed the door to the balcony was ajar. Her feet tingled as she stepped toward the door. It had been closed, she was sure, yet perhaps she forgot, perhaps in a dream she had closed it.

Everything in the room was as it should be: flowered couch, sepia photographs, framed lace, the empty birdcage hanging from the spotted ceiling. They lay in thrift shops and alleyways waiting for her.

Alice ran to the bedroom but the bureau remained untouched. The bed in the blue corner was still made. Alice crouched near it, lifting the sides of the bedspread to peer underneath. She pushed clothes aside in closets and looked behind the bathroom door. When she stood still to listen, she heard only the faint sounds of a television. An old couple from upstairs who stayed in most days. Once when Alice brought their groceries up for them, the old man touched her breast.

A knocking. She stood before the heavy brown door.

'Alice?' Moira's voice.

She unlocked the door but forgot about the chain. When she pulled the door she could see Moira through the gap in the door. Then she was inside wondering why Alice put the chain on during the day.

One night she put a pile of boxes and books against the door; if someone should break in, she would hear, but the cats knocked it all over in the middle of the night, while she slept soundly.

Alice took Moira's shawl still warm and perfumed to the bedroom. When she returned, Moira was moving about the room, her long skirt whispering against the wooden floor. 'I feel I've stepped into your private world. Everything fits together so perfectly.'

Alice blushed under Moira's gaze. It was as if she noticed something Alice had forgotten to hide. She busied herself with the kettle while Moira sat down before cups and saucers.

Moira's bracelets shook as she raised the teacup to her lips. Alice liked to look at her, especially her eyes so large and soft.

They moved to the couch, resting their teacups on a tiny stool. 'Did you hear about the rape? Yesterday I think. A woman living alone not far from here. That's what they said.'

Alice nodded, wondering if she should mention the balcony door. Then it would become real.

'I get so nervous when I hear these stories. I'm paranoid, I know,' Moira said.

Alice stared down at her empty teacup. 'It's natural to be afraid of such things.'

'But I take chances. I meet some guy in a bar. How do I know who he really is?'

'You must get some enjoyment out of it.'

'But it's not like what I have with you or my other women friends.' Moira looked at her. 'Do you have fears?'

'You mean fear of death,' Alice began, 'yes, sometimes, but more...' The cripple so young his mouth moving at her. 'But more I fear spiritual death.'

'Yes that's what it feels like when I'm too listless to rise.' Moira fell silent, her eyes half closed. 'And if that death was near, what would you do?'

'I'd ask God.'

Moira reached for her teacup. 'I didn't think anyone believed. Are you one of those born again people?'

Alice wanted to bring her back. 'I'm a Catholic.'

That seemed to explain something to Moira. 'You're lucky to find such comfort.'

But it could not be otherwise. To wake fatherless, her body suspended in night air, to kneel alone in the dark funnel of the church. 'Are you so alone?'

Moira started to speak, then shook her head. She reached out and put her arms around Alice.

Inside her warm body, Alice felt weak, her arms and legs seemed to dissolve. Her heart was burning, and the air filled with the scent of musk and earth. She felt she might stop breathing. When she made a slight movement away, Moira released her.

Moira looked at her and away as if she too was ashamed. Alice offered more tea, but Moira was leaving soon. She was seeing a new man she'd met in the One Hand Bookstore.

After she left, Alice sipped her tea till the room darkened. Then she made a salad and worked on her essay till late. She lit a candle and began her yoga on the living room floor.

With her back straight, her legs crossed, her hands upturned on her knees, she chanted 'Shantih, Shantih.' Alice began to feel lighter, as if her heart had stilled itself. With her eyes shut she lay on her belly, grasped her heels and rocked back and forth. Her body warmed; she pulled her legs up higher till her muscles strained. She thought of Moira, of her warm flesh and waited for the thought to pass as other thoughts as passed out of her in yoga class. She strained further, rocked more quickly. She was touching Moira's breasts as a man would.

Alice opened her eyes. The candle burned beside her. The empty birdcage cast a huge shadow on the ceiling. She carried the candle into the bedroom, pulled down the shade to hide the fire escape and climbed into bed. She listened. A tapping from a radiator like an impatient foot. She reached out in the darkness and blew out the candle, then drew the covers over her arms, waiting for the outline of the room to become clear again.

creeping down the room hands touching walls ceiling window
lifting the shade away she sees him staring up
quickly quickly she lets go has he seen

she dresses in dim light her hair pulled back
the search with hands and eyes for marks lines for traces

on the bridge figures approach recede pale faces
she looks away in windows he passes with a smile
pressing against his thinness an empty bag

long bright lights her desk a neat square
her hands flat on the top her eyes closed
here he could not find her

is there anything wrong he asks
she cranes her neck to see
his head become light specks whirling through darkness
curtains parting to reveal

nothing I was dizzy all of a sudden

black letters moving across a gleaming page his face

eyes lowered he will not see me will fade into the city
he approaches stops her feet aching to run his mouth moving
she hurries on he knows he knows he knows
will wait outside my window
shake the lock of my door as I sleep

where are you
her hands reach in darkness his shadow fills her eyes

Robert sits side saddle on his wooden pedestal by the cash register watching for thieves and pretty women. He's never caught anyone stealing books, but the women fall readily into his arms. The One Hand Bookstore is on what Robert calls the only funky street in Denver. Rangy trees shade the cracked sidewalk, the houses from Molly Brown's time, the drugstore with a soda fountain where an ancient soda jerk mixes vanilla Cokes. On summer days when the boxy downtown burns in dry heat, readers shade their eyes as they emerge from the perpetual dusk of the bookstore.

Everything seems to lean in the store: the rough wooden shelves braced by sloping walls, the floor rising to the backroom where readers sit in warped pews torn from a ghost town church. The spiritual books live in the backroom; the front is devoted to the real world of fiction and poetry. It's a librarian's nightmare: Ginsberg alongside Whitman, Keats with Homer, *Tom Jones* and *On the Road*.

'Look for affinities,' Robert tells the bewildered customers.

Robert is small when he climbs down from his pedestal, a compact man with straight black hair emerging from a widow's peak, large blue eyes with a look of wonder and thin protruding lips. One of his girlfriends called him a handsome frog.

Robert manages the store, but his friend Mudra owns it. They met up in Boulder, the two of them the only reliable members of a commune. It was Robert who finally scraped the chocolate fondue from the living room floor, Mudra who paid the telephone bills. When they moved out, Mudra to a Buddhist community and Robert to the first of his semi-furnished apartments down in Denver, they told each other that the bookstore would be the real commune.

Mudra practices blankness. He is a long person with an ascetic horse face and a ponytail. When he's not contemplating the blue void, he reads Sikh stories to himself. Mudra's real name is George Johnson Junior and the store feeds off his father's pharmaceutical company in Chicago.

They keep the One Hand so dark that customers have to peer at the books to see the titles. It's as hushed as the opening of a church service. Over in the corner behind a display of books on Taoism, a man is standing on his head. He comes in every day and has scared away some women for he strips down to his boxer shorts before taking up his position. This Mudra will tolerate, but not the thieves who rob him of what little profit he can make. He does not understand how it happens for the two of them watch over the rooms and secretly he has even looked through Robert's knapsack. Yet the stock totals and sales do not tally.

Robert keeps a pad and pencil handy; after he has spied a woman and then engaged her at the cash register, he asks her to write down her telephone number. He always whispers as if planning an adulterous tryst, but Robert has never been married. For six months he lived with a woman he described ever after as 'a dramatic Jewish beauty'.

'It's all passing me by,' he complained.

'What's the "it"?' asked the dramatic Jewish beauty.

'Life.' He waved his arms about, but he meant the women who walked past the cash register each day. Marriage would be like reading the same book for eternity. Yet he longs to fall in love.

She had come in before, a delicate woman with cat's eyes who shed her coat to reveal bare arms in winter, her hair in a shiny braid. Robert decides she has oriental blood. He notices she spends her time at the poetry section but hasn't talked to her for she never buys and always seems to glide past him just as he's ringing up a sale. He catches Mudra's eye, beckons and then climbs down from his stool. Mudra sighs but takes Robert's place. Robert walks over to the poetry section and pretends to be rearranging books near her. He makes a big show of looking at each book before replacing it on the shelf. She ignores him at first but as he gets closer, he knows she's watching.

'You need a flashlight in here,' she says.

'Don't you find it soothing?'

'If you want to sleep.' She continues to look through the books as she talks, pulls out a volume of Sappho. He watches with despair as she calmly turns the pages, is relieved when after a few minutes she puts it back in the wrong place next to Shelley.

'Excuse me,' he says touching her bare shoulder as he reaches across to put Sappho next to Amy Lowell.

She watches him. 'How do you remember?'

'Oh you do.'

He decides she is going to be difficult for the mood has not changed between them. He could just as well be up on his pedestal.

'So you're into poetry.'

She looks bored as if this approach has been made before and begins fingering books.

'Do you write yourself?'

She turns towards him, her face suddenly shy.

'You know about our poetry workshop?' he says.

'I'm just a beginner.'

'Everyone is.'

She gives him a look.

One of the poets is reading from a steno pad while the others in the semi-circle of pews nod their heads. She tells them about her affair with her boss, the slice of pie they share afterwards, before he goes home to his wife. 'But you, you don't remember,' is the poem's refrain.

She walks in late, 'the oriental', so Robert names her, and sits down alone in the outer circle of pews. The others shift in their seats; they're not used to strangers.

'Come inside,' says the beat poet, opening his arms wide and emitting the smell of unwashed wool.

She shakes her head. 'I've nothing to read.'

The beat poet winks at her. 'This is another one of my odes,' he says, 'to my Rocky Mountain lover.'

81

Robert clutches the seat to keep from hitting him as he declaims in a nasal voice: 'Moon face girl, give me the night, the liquid night. Let me show you God. Oh God! Your thighs.'

A man with eyes of a nocturnal animal recites one of his television poems while the other poets wait their turn, their moist hands holding thin sheets. For some reason they favor onionskin, except for the beat poet who composes his stringy poems on pieces of cardboard.

Robert has felt some affection towards these innocents struggling to invent themselves, but now he wants to shake himself free. As he walks her home he tells her they were terrible. She says she doesn't know much about poetry. She's an art student, but doesn't say where. Cynthia Williams. Robert continues to think of her as 'the oriental'.

At Colfax cars rumble up the hill without stopping. Cynthia runs across. 'Don't do that,' he says as he steps into traffic holding up his arms. But she walks on, and he follows her down a narrow street till they reach a sagging yellow clapboard house where she rents a one-room flat. After she leaves him, he waits outside the house for a minute. Just to make sure, he thinks, just that. He hears shouting. The door opens and a woman in an orange bathrobe runs out, then down the street towards Colfax. The light switches on in the top floor; a man's face appears in the window, severe and still as a death mask. As Robert turns away, he sees the woman stagger back weeping.

'Stop staring!' she shouts.

He points to himself with a questioning look and feels like a child at school. But she has already slammed the door behind her. Soon after the window goes dark and the house is quiet. Pale and specter thin, the ladies of the evening pass Robert on Colfax, their long coats open to reveal halter-tops and hot pants. He runs the rest of the way home.

He paces his rooms unable to sleep, then takes out a sheaf of papers. He's been reworking one page of writing for two years, a story about the last inning in a baseball game, someone stealing third base. He decides to begin again.

'Look alive,' Mudra says as he swings by the cash register. Robert is startled to see his friend's face so close. He's been daydreaming again about Cynthia.

He's never seen Mudra so upset. He thinks an expensive book of photographs of the Himalayas has gone walking. There was only one copy and neither of them remembers selling it. Mudra's father is threatening to pull out of the store if they can't show a good profit.

A whole week has passed since the poetry evening, and somehow Robert has not got around to asking Cynthia out. She unnerves him with her cool smile, her noiseless movements.

Mudra calls her 'the snake woman'. 'She's not all there. I can sense these things,' he says solemnly as they close the store. Robert ignores his warning; long ago he decided that Mudra has never tasted a woman.

They're sitting in the dim room beyond the horseshoe bar of the Oak Alley eating enchiladas and filling their glasses from a pitcher of yellow beer. The black ceiling is studded with silver. Robert imagines himself out in an open field with her, the sky like a glittering blanket over their naked bodies. It's the closest he's ever come to writing poetry.

She wears a black knitted shell, her sallow arms bare as usual. 'Aren't you cold?' He puts his arm around her. Such skin she has, like fine silk, like the night bedding he imagines.

The beer seems to release her from cryptic one-liners. She tells him her mother was Japanese, her father an American soldier stationed in Japan after the war. When they came back to live in Denver, the father's hometown, the mother languished. She could not eat American food; the hamburgers doused with ketchup and the large potatoes oozing butter offended her. She asked her family back in Japan to send dried seaweed, soybean paste and flat noodles. Cynthia remembers sitting at the table with the two of them, her father chewing bloody meat, her mother with a plate of translucent noodles.

Robert orders another pitcher of beer. And what about her, what did she eat?

She spreads her narrow hands. They fed her meat and potatoes to make her a strong American girl, but she threw up afterwards. When her mother wasn't looking she took handfuls of her noodles and ate them uncooked, for Cynthia was too young to know what to do with the tangle of white sticks. 'I'm still weird about red meat.'

After this confession, Robert tells her about the baseball story which he's never shown to anyone but Mudra. When they reach his apartment, two barren rooms in a cavernous red brick apartment building, she asks to see it. She lights up a cigarette, sits before the roll-top desk reading the latest version.

'Don't scrutinize it,' he says, his hands on her shoulders.

She brushes the smoke away from her face, looks around for an ashtray. Normally Robert berates people for smoking, but now he dutifully brings her a saucer and watches her tip in the ashes. He's read somewhere that you could tell a lot about a person by the way they snuff out a cigarette. She makes a perfunctory effort, then leaves the butt still burning. He sighs, reaches over and grinds the cigarette into the saucer.

Cynthia turns from the desk to stare at him, raises her arms. He's confused for a moment. Is she just stretching, does she want him to bend down and kiss her or is she asking to be carried to bed? He decides on the latter.

Cynthia's so small and fragile, he feels he can't quite grasp her. She seems to slip through his arms like a shadow. Afterwards he wanders into the bathroom and under the eye of the bare bulb discovers that his girlfriend from the night before has left her diaphragm in full view.

When Robert returns to the bedroom Cynthia has turned on the light and begun dressing.

'Something wrong?' He assumes she's seen the diaphragm, why she's leaving in a huff.

But she just smiles up at him. 'I've got an early class tomorrow.'

'I'll walk you.'

'Don't bother.'

He doesn't insist. He's woozy from it all: their silent love-making followed by the discovery of the diaphragm and the flash of the bedroom light when they should be sleeping. He feels like he's been shaken from a dream. He staggers down the stairs after her, watches from the doorway as she walks towards the lighted dome of Capitol Hill.

Mudra is growing desperate. At stocktaking they discover the store has lost a hundred dollars' worth of books in one week. The thief is wrecking his life: when Mudra meditates, he sees the blue void through empty bookshelves. He looks sideways at Robert and wonders aloud if there's been some conspiracy.

Robert listens but can't seem to achieve the vigilant mood Mudra demands. He finds himself thinking of Cynthia when he should be paying attention to the words of others. Yesterday he did not answer when a woman asked him repeatedly for the *I Ching*. He was sitting at his post, chin in hand staring beyond her moving lips.

'Is anyone home?' she shouted in his ear.

Mudra is saying they will have to force people to check their bags.

'But they won't like it. You'll spoil the atmosphere.'

'They all do it now,' Mudra says.

'But we're not them.'

Mudra looks away from Robert. For once his horse face has an earthly expression. There is sadness in his large eyes. 'It's the only way.'

At first Robert lets his friends go by without asking them to check their knapsacks, but Mudra insists on everyone. They put up a sign and erect some shelves for bags behind the cash register.

'Jesus, what've you got in there?' He lifts Cynthia's knapsack over the counter.

'Paints and stuff.'

When she turns her back, he opens the knapsack and discovers a chicken and a large bag of rice. He thinks the paints must be hidden underneath all that and does not look further.

By the end of the week when they check the stock, they discover only fifteen dollars' worth of books missing.

'It must be working,' Mudra says but he doesn't look happy.

'You mean you want to continue?'

'We've got to.'

Robert feels his position has changed. No longer is he muse of the bookstore. The new customers regard him as they would a security guard in a department store. The regulars often forget to check their bags; when he calls them back, his voice booming over the hush of the store, they heave their knapsacks over the counter in disgust.

He's surprised at how violent he begins to feel towards the thief who even now has managed to shove a few books under his coat. Mudra thinks there must be several thieves but Robert suspects the beat poet who has taken to wearing a kaftan.

In the evening he takes Cynthia to the Electric Folk Club. It's after midnight when they emerge. He walks her home but she does not ask him in. He feels he has to pass some test before he's allowed entrance. But weeks pass and always it is his apartment where they make love and then separate, for Cynthia confesses that she cannot sleep with someone else in the bed.

'It's something I'm trying to work out,' she tells him.

She's afraid to get involved, and this Robert can understand. But he feels uneasy. Perhaps Cynthia changes as she sleeps into someone she can't control and when she wakes in the morning from such dreams, she is not so beautiful. Even alone she does not sleep well for there are shadows about her watchful eyes.

She says money worries keep her awake. Her parents are divorced; her mother lives alone in a high rise built as reparation to the Japanese Americans interned during the war. Her father travels around Wyoming selling cattle medicine. Cynthia lives on government student loans and food stamps, and buys her clothes from the Salvation Army. She's so immaculate that Robert cannot imagine her picking through dresses smelling of other women.

When he does not see her in the store for a week, Robert phones but gets no answer. As he puts down the receiver, he thinks she should not live alone in such a rough house. He's surprised by his concern, for normally his girlfriends do not preoccupy him. He decides to visit her on his day off.

The place depresses him in daylight with its front yard strewn with garbage and broken glass, but inside the little hallway is surprisingly neat and clean. Cynthia comes to the door in a short kimono with a pattern of cherry blossoms. Her black hair is loose and she's barefoot. He's reminded of the willing Polynesian girl in *South Pacific*.

'I've been sick.' She continues to stand by the door.

He wonders if she will let him in. He offers to buy her food.

She shakes her head. 'Can't hold anything down. I got some kind of bug.'

'Can I come in?'

She looks at him warily. 'Well, okay, if you want to catch it.'

'Not if you don't want me to.'

'You might as well.'

Outside is a bright relentless Denver day, the sky above the glass towers pure sapphire, but she lives in dusk. With the heavy curtains drawn and the high ceiling, her narrow room resembles a tomb.

'You've been sleeping?'

'I never pull the curtains. I'm on the ground floor. You get people looking in.'

He sits down on the one chair, a rocker, while she lies across the bed. He feels uncomfortable under her silent gaze and walks over to look at her books.

'Don't scrutinize,' she says.

He turns around with a smile, but she stares at him. 'Are any of these from the One Hand?'

'Maybe. Maybe a few.'

Yes they are familiar, his stock, and he doesn't think about what she said till he notices the book about the Himalayas. As he opens it up he sees the stock card still inside. He keeps his back to her as his eyes cloud with tears. He cannot speak but simply flashes the card at her over his shoulder.

'They forgot to take it out.'

'They?' His voice shakes. 'They?' The stock card is clearly marked with their stamp, a mandala superimposed by the palm of a hand. He puts the book back on the shelf with care as if he were in the One Hand.

The room is still. When he finally turns around, she's sitting up in bed, her fingers combing her hair.

'Why d'you steal from me?'

'Because it was so easy.'

'But why?'

'I can't afford to buy them.'

'You know I'd lend them to you if you only asked.'

'They're more your own when you steal them.'

'I just don't believe it.' He sits down on the edge of the bed. When she touches his neck he shivers.

'Sorry. I got poor circulation,' she says.

'That's why you never invited me in.' He presses his forehead hard as if to force the discovery into his brain.

'You're going to take them back?' She does not even seem afraid he will tell Mudra or call in the police.

'I don't know.'

He hears a sigh and wants to shake her but keeps his back turned.

'Why me? Why steal from me?'

'I didn't think you'd care. You don't even own the store.'

'But Mudra does. He's my friend and besides—' He breaks off realizing that she does not understand the sanctity of the bookstore.

'I'm sorry,' she says, but getting no absolution from him, she confesses, 'You're not the only one.'

'Wonderful.'

'It's the way I got to live. I think why should I pay when I can slip a steak into my bag?'

He turns around. 'I thought you didn't like steak.'

'I don't but—' She lies back on the bed, her face exhausted.

Something about this movement of resignation touches Robert. It is as if she has finally given herself to him.

'Can I steal you?' he whispers in the gloom. He bends over her body. 'Can I?'

THE BORDERS OF MY SELF

She remembered her with the color yellow. Not the brilliance of a child's sun, but the shade of ageing walls, Tamar's face when she opened the door after a silent bell.

Joseph sat in the living room holding a large magnifying glass before a dismembered watch. So deaf that he did not look up till Anna and her mother drew close. 'When you get old like me, you shrink. Your grandma said so. Do you see me shrinking?' But Anna couldn't remember a time when he wasn't a small old man with fine white hair and full pink lips.

On her birthday Joseph gave her a kaleidoscope. 'You look through and you see what really is,' he said. 'Like Einstein you become.' The doilies on the crimson sofa whirled, her grandfather's soft face shattered as she twisted the rim at the end of the black cardboard tube. Later when they reached home, Anna's mother called the kaleidoscope a cheap toy. Why did her parents shame her?

They had tea there: Anna, her mother and grandmother. Grandpa Joseph was never invited into the kitchen. Sylvia was always in a hurry so Tamar cooled the teas with water from the sink, the film on the brownish liquid like an oily puddle. But Anna drank her tea, for when she finished she knew it would be time to leave.

Her mother could not be Tamar's daughter, this Anna knew. Grandma Tamar, a tall sallow woman with lips like a broken sore. Sylvia's face bright with lipstick and glossy black pencil, her talk loud, but in her mother's house she was content to give glances instead of words. The lifting of the eyebrows, the head tilted to one side meant: 'Don't worry, we'll be going soon. We were going when we came.'

Until she was seven, Anna wasn't allowed on her own beyond the stoop. Strangers with long arms might snatch her. But down in the basement past the sourness of the tin barrels lived a woman whose face she had never seen for she rushed by so fast. Ellen had glimpsed a pointed chin, the peak of a red scarf before the witch woman went into the darkness of the basement which contained her, a darkness Anna had touched with the tips of her hands. Once she and Ellen had begun to walk down those stairs but Anna, hearing the sound of mumbling, had run away.

'She's not a witch,' Sylvia said, 'just very, very sad.'

'Why?' asked Anna.

'She came over from the other side and she misses her friends.'

On the other side people cried in a forest where children were eaten and great dogs roamed free. The other side was a place where badness lived but sometimes it was an old place, so old that everyone slept beneath frowsy trees.

'What's her name?'

'Mrs Wasser. Something like that. You leave her alone. You and that Ellen. You're troublemakers.'

'I never did anything.'

'I don't want you teasing or talking to her.'

'Why? What's wrong with her?'

But Sylvia Brenner was dialing a number on the telephone. And when she began talking she gestured to Anna, a backward flip of the hand, to go away.

Anna sat down on the sofa and propped her doll on a cushion. The sun was throwing fairy dust through the window and she caught the gold and red in her hands. When she turned from the light, her doll was staring at her.

'What's the matter?' Her father arrived, his heavy coat containing the cold from the street down below her tower window. 'Why does she just sit there like that?'

'Stop moping.' Sylvia stood in front of Anna.

Anna shivered and turned her head.

'What is it?' her mother asked with more gentleness.

Anna shook her head. She couldn't tell her mother that she heard another woman speak suddenly in a voice that screeched like a subway train when they went downtown.

Her father came forward, his coat still on and grabbed Anna

by the wrist, tore her from the sofa. 'You snap out of it.'

'Look what you've done,' Sylvia said. Anna had crawled back on the sofa, and lay face down, crying into the shiny slipcover.

'She's getting like your mother,' Saul said.

'Don't say "your mother".'

'You know what I mean.'

They were shouting at each other, but it was not so bad as night time when the light from the living room flared in the open spaces around Anna's shut door. Her doll was running ahead of her around the room, around and around. Anna grabbed at the long black yarn hair but the doll pulled away, its red cloth mouth alive with laughter. Then she was chasing Anna, chasing her up through waking.

Anna reached the bottom of the stairway just as the witch was entering the building. She held a large wicker basket, the twisted handle in the crook of her arm. Anna had never seen anything like it before. All the mothers carried large brown bags or wheeled grey metal carts full of food.

She drew back the plaid cover on her basket and picked out an orange. 'Take.' Her low voice did not match the words which sounded like a command to Anna. She wanted to run but the woman stood in her path holding the poisoned fruit.

'I can't,' Anna whispered, 'my mother told me not to take from strangers.'

'So,' the woman said, putting the orange back in the basket next to a pale green cabbage. 'So that's the way it is here.'

She moved past Anna. 'Goodbye little girl.' Her sigh was the first Anna remembered hearing, a fine sad sound like wind through bare trees.

Her mother did not hear her anymore and when Anna asked for a story, Sylvia said, 'I'll tell you a story of Mary and Mory. And now my story's begun. I'll tell you another about her brother and now my story is done.'

'But that's not a story.'

'Yes it is.'

'Not a real story.'

'Shush.'

Sylvia's body swelled so that she could not tie her own shoes; like a turtle she was, her belly a shell she did not like touched.

Anna was sitting with her father in the maroon leather booth in Jack's. She watched the foam grow on her malted milk before inserting her straw. Jack had poured it himself from a silver shaker to the tall fluted glass. She had never had a soda there with her father.

'Thanks chief,' Saul said to Jack.

'Seven already,' Jack was saying about her. And then he went back behind the counter to read his newspaper.

When her father told her she would have to stay with Grandma Tamar and Grandpa Joseph, she could not finish her soda. The straw was ruined, sucked flat and dry. 'Only for a few days,' he said. Then Saul gave her a nickel to buy the penny candies. Sometimes Jack got mad at the children who hovered around the glass case of liquorice shoelace, chocolate babies, wax lips, teeth and noses which when chewed gave off a sweet perfume. Anna chose five of her favorites: a cerise candy lipstick in gold foil. She unwrapped one, licked the end and spread the red stain on her lips, making her mouth as bright as her mother's.

'Junk,' her father said as he watched her bite into the soft chalky stick, its brilliant color dimming as she reached the center.

As they walked to the door, Saul stopped to talk to Jack who came from behind the newspapers and chewing gum, the glass barrel of pretzel sticks. Suddenly Jack picked her up and she was close to his broad freckled face and flame-colored hair, and he bounced her as if she was a baby while she fought to get free. It was brighter up there, high above the counter, the light shone on dull glass cabinets, on the rows of metal shakers, on the spotted mirror.

'What a skinny kid!' Jack said to her father who was

laughing, patting Jack on the back. 'She's nothing like her mother. Like you maybe.' Jack scrutinized the two of them, now on the same level, shook his head. Then she was down on her feet in the dim space between them.

Anna sucked on the lipstick. Whatever was in her mother's belly would be a round person like her mother. And she was being sent to a place where no one could find her.

Grandma Tamar put Anna in a room at the back of the apartment. 'Junk,' she muttered as she set a wooden box filled with toys on the floor near the narrow bed. 'What your mother and her brother used to play with. You'll find something, no?'

Nothing was whole. Beneath a rubble of wooden blocks, broken rattles and watch faces, lay a soft rubber dolly grey with age whose eyes and mouth had become faint smudges. Near her she discovered a small cloth doll with green eyes, frayed yellow braids and a full red skirt; if she turned the doll upside down and pulled the skirt down to cover the smiling face, there was another doll, a white-haired bespectacled woman with a stern face. Though she knew they could not leave each other, Anna tried to pull the dolls apart.

She did not want to sleep with the box of toys in her room, but could not say that to Tamar who came in to turn off her light and left without a word. Anna held her own doll against her chest under the covers. The double doll appeared when she shut her eyes, so she stared up at the patterns formed on the ceiling by light coming through the venetian blinds, stripes of grey which moved as the blinds swayed in the wind.

Long after her grandparents switched off all the lights in the apartment, she heard Tamar's footsteps, up and down in the hallway past Anna's room. Then a door opened and shut and all was still. Though the city lay around the apartment, Anna heard no noise from the street, only from inside the body of the building, the gulping of the elevator.

Grandpa left early to work at the store where he repaired clocks and watches. 'Sometimes for rich gentlemen,' he told Anna.

'Greenhorn,' Tamar said. 'You left the other side. Remember? There's no gentlemen here.'

After he left Tamar stood for a long time in the middle of the living room, looking as if she was trying to remember something she'd lost. Anna sat on the sofa sucking her thumb, but Tamar did not pull it out of her mouth. The ringing of the telephone stirred her, and she walked slowly to the kitchen to answer it. She was talking for a long time, and then Anna heard the sound of water flowing, plates and cups from breakfast being washed and put away. She pulled her thumb out of her mouth and made a bridal veil for her doll out of a doily which lay on the arm of Grandpa's easy chair.

In the playground, Tamar sat on the bench just like Anna's mother did while Anna fled to the monkey bars. Tamar did not shout out, 'Be careful!' or tell her to stay on the low bars. She did not even glance in Anna's direction.

Anna began to climb to the top; she looked back, expecting an anxious expression on her grandmother's face, a hand raised in protest, but Tamar had shut her eyes. She continued to climb upwards, something she never did, for hadn't her mother told her about the little girl who cracked her head falling from the top of the monkey bars? 'Then who can climb there?' Anna had asked.

She was sitting at the top now, swinging her legs in the air, but there was no one to see her so she climbed down. Tamar was far away, a still old woman lost in dreams.

Anna was used to playing alone. She had Ellen Fischer from the building and Debby who stood in front of her when they went size place in line from recess, but nobody else, not really. Her father thought it was because she was too smart for the other girls. 'You're in with the dummies,' he liked to say. But Anna knew it was because she did not talk or run around the room when the teacher left the class like the other girls did. And during recess, when the bigger boys forced all the girls to sit on the benches with their hands crossed, she remained seated, her hands trembling even after everyone had gotten up and run away. But she hated the boys more than the other girls did, and this she could not hide from them, how she wanted to make them shrivel and die.

Anna stood in the middle of the playground wondering where to go next: the sliding-pond covered with yellow leaves, the faded lines of the hopscotch squares. There was no one to watch her throw the stick, to see her complete a journey through the squares, only strange girls who said 'Staring at something?' when she drew close.

Anna stood up on the wooden seat of the swing, something she could be slapped for. She pumped herself by bending her knees and stretching her chest forward till her body flew through the air and only the fence around the playground reminded her that she was not in flight to the very tops of the crimson apartment buildings. Then she came down slowly in a flood of nausea and sat down on the swing. A boy stared at her from the top of the sliding-pond, but the other children had gone home to lunch when the siren had sounded noon.

The solitary woman on the bench had disappeared, the old one, Tamar, had left with the others. And Anna did not know the way home. She waited for her to appear, to come back when she remembered her granddaughter, but the playground's silence did not hold her. Anna ran outside the gate but did not find Tamar on the narrow path edged with prickly bushes; further on she ran but Tamar was not sitting with the old men and women facing the yellowish grass, or walking with the mothers, the slow gait of women pushing hooded carriages, talking about secrets.

Anna returned to the playground but her grandmother was not there shaking a fist at her for wandering away. She ran out the back gates which led to a stone stairway half hidden by a low brick wall. Tamar stood below in a tunnel formed by trees and the fronts of buildings, her back that of a stranger's.

'Grandma,' Anna called out when she had descended the stairs, afraid that like a long cloud she would drift off. Tamar turned, stared without surprise, without anger, at the child who disturbed her.

'What do you want?'

'I was scared you went away.'

'I can't go away.' Tamar began to pace back and forth, then to walk in a circle. She sat down on one of the stoops, the thick brown arm of a squat building, with her hands flat on her knees. Anna stood near, then sat in the same position on the other brown arm. She did not speak until the chill from the trees lay on her skin.

'I wanna go home.'

Tamar did not speak, did not even turn her head. A woman passed pulling an empty grey shopping cart and stared at Tamar with a smile like a mean puppet's.

'Grandma!' Anna shouted. Tamar stood up, began walking, this time slowly and with direction.

'When I was your age, yes it must have been, or was I older? How old are you?' But before Anna could answer she went on: 'I forget when. I started working in my father's shop.'

'Was that around here?'

'No, no. In Lublin of course. I worked behind the counter, fetching cloth and ribbons all day. It was a little shop, dark and narrow, a small stove only for heating. In the winter I used to hop up and down so that my feet were not lost to the cold. It was a shop for poor people. My father talked about moving to a rich part of the town, but he never did. He used to shout. How frightened I was of his temper. Now I think he was just a small old man, smaller even than Joseph. But then his voice was like a hammer beating me down. I wanted to go to school but he could only afford to send my brothers.'

Anna listened in wonder. Her grandmother's dry mouth had never spoken so many words.

'On Fridays I helped my mother cook for Shabbes. She wanted everything just so. Only on Saturday, on Shabbes, was I free, but then I had to be quiet and still. One morning I ran away early before my parents woke up, before even my brothers began dressing for school. I thought I'd take a ship to America.' She laughed.

'What's so funny?' Anna asked, thinking, she's laughing at me.

'There's no water. You see, we have only land around us.

You must go for miles to find a port. So I searched all day for something that wasn't. But I was so shy I couldn't ask anyone. And then the darkness came quickly, and the cold. A boy chased me till I was lost and had to ask the way home. My father hit me hard but I know he cried.'

They continued to walk but in silence. Then Tamar asked, 'So what do you think? You have a brother now.' She looked at Anna with bright eyes. 'Your mother will be too busy for you. What do you think of that?'

The next morning Tamar did not leave her bedroom. Grandpa Joseph made Anna a breakfast of fried egg and toasted rye bread. Anna was making the gleaming surface of the yolk tremble with her fork when he said, 'Grandma doesn't feel well today. You'll come with me to the store.'

She broke the yellow eye with her knife and looked up at him. 'What's wrong with her?'

'She's tired. Her head is hurting.' He patted Anna's hair and kissed her cheek; for once his soft lips did not repel her. But the sick air made Anna too nauseous to eat her egg. Grandpa brought a pot of dark coffee to the round table. He ate nothing but drank two cups of the chocolate ink whose smell filled the kitchen, pushing away the odor from her grandmother's bedroom, and the throw-up went back down Anna's throat.

Joseph worked in the back room of Weiss's jewellery store on a wide, treeless street where cars rumbled up and down all day. At the very top of the hill, past the narrow room of Jacoby, the upholsterer, past the stained velvet sofas sitting outside Low's Used Furniture, past the store without a name which sold the missing parts of radios, the sky was riven by the black rails of the elevated train. As Anna sat with her grandfather in the small room, she could hear the low thunder of the trains. He worked at a long narrow table covered in brown paper, the sharp light beside him focussed on the watch which lay with its head open in his hand. His thick glasses were not thick enough, so he held a magnifying glass above the still wheels.

Anna had brought her doll and a book but she watched

her grandfather work. She didn't move or speak for the least whisper could send the tiny wheels flying. Joseph's lips were pursed, his eyes searching from behind all the magnification for a broken part. He reminded her of the dentist, picking up and exchanging one sharp instrument for another, his serious face bent over her mouth.

'So,' he mumbled and a smile spread his lips. His hands against the paper on the table made a low rough sound like the fingers of the woman in the musty heat of the Chinese laundry, wrapping her mother's sheets in brown paper. When Joseph had finished two watches, he filled up the pipe which lay beside him, lit it, sucked in the smoke and closed his eyes. Then he removed the pipe from his mouth and asked Anna if she was not bored.

For lunch they went to the delicatessen where a man with a broad fleshy face, a white cap pinned to the back of his head, was frying potato knishes and hot dogs. In the front window painted with a large white Jewish star hung purple salamis, huge necklaces of hot dogs and a calendar with a picture of a desert.

'Did you hear? I have a grandson,' he told the man.

The man continued to turn the knishes, but he said, 'He should bring *naches* to you.'

'What?'

'*Naches*, I said he should bring.'

'Yes, yes,' Joseph mumbled and he took Anna's hand and led her to one of the tables.

Anna had a hot dog with mustard and sauerkraut, and a dill pickle. She knew she could have the food her parents said was junk. Joseph wouldn't skim off some of the sauerkraut and take half of the pickle, to stop her getting a bellyache.

After his sandwich, Grandpa sipped a glass of golden brown tea. 'I thought you didn't like tea,' Anna said. He did not appear to have heard so she repeated herself.

'Why should you think that?'

'When we come to visit you never drink tea with us.'

Grandpa spoke to himself in the language from the other

102

side. 'Stop speaking "Jewish". Nobody understands,' her mother always said to him.

'What does that mean?' Anna asked.

He looked angry but not at Anna. 'Your grandma doesn't ask and even so. She does not make tea the way I'm used to.' Before she could ask more questions, he drank down the rest of his tea, wiped his mouth with a stiff paper napkin and beckoned her to rise.

As they stood facing the cars careening down the hill, waiting for the lights to change, Anna thought he looked like the old man her mother once helped over an icy sidewalk. When he took her hand to cross, Anna felt she was guiding him for he was so downcast he did not look where he was going.

When he was back in his chair in front of the pile of watches, his eyes had a faraway look. Anna asked him for a story.

'I don't have any.'

'Please.'

'I'll tell you about my city.' He shut his eyes for he was drawing pictures in his mind, and when he was full of the colors of the past he told her about the bridges with their stone statues and lacework of iron which lay across the silken river, the turrets and bell towers, the spires twisting in the wind.

When she asked what a turret was, he drew one in pencil on the thick brown paper covering the table, and then she knew he had come from a place of castles.

When he walked down the streets of his city, he heard music, for someone was singing or playing the violin in their room or an orchestra was performing. Late at night snow filled the windows of the ancient houses, muffled the footfalls of men leaving the taverns and the clopping of horses, till the silence was broken by the chiming of the old town clock which never stopped no matter what happened. A woman lived in the clock.

'Everyone knew about her. We said she was a Jewish spirit, a dybbuk who had not found a body and fled to the dark tower.'

'What's a dybbuk?'

'But haven't I just said? Well, you may hear this and that. Every Jew has his own explanation, but I think it is a soul gone wrong, and not only a Jewish soul. Instead of flying up to God, for it is not a bad soul, you see, the dybbuk searches all the time on earth for a home, a body to possess. Maybe it died with its work half-finished, or was silenced before it could speak. They say the spirit of a bridegroom once possessed a tailor and forced him to stitch up his wedding suit. The dybbuks are all the time nagging at us to remember. Sometimes you can hear them weep and moan; when we refuse to listen, when we say it was the sound of gates not oiled or entangled trees, they grow wicked with anger.'

Anna grew confused and lost interest in the low voice repeating a word she could not pronounce. He was not speaking to her anymore.

'But I have forgotten the clock tower. You see when the hour struck, a procession of saints appeared through a door at the front of the clock followed by an angel with a trumpet in one hand and a sword in the other. But for all that it was a sad angel not a fiery one. I thought it was the spirit of the dead woman made it so, telling the angel stories from her life. She had been married against her will to a fool, a man who bought her beauty and her eager mind from her poor parents, as if she were not a live thing, a person. He kept her away from everyone, afraid she would run off. But when she did leave him in the only way she could, he did not mourn long.'

Joseph tapped Anna on the head as if to alert her that now the good part was coming. 'Late in the night when the clock struck three, the angel became possessed, no longer sad, it began to wave its sword and blow its trumpet; the woman danced her freedom from within the stone body of the angel.'

'Did you see that?'

Joseph smiled and squeezed Anna's arm. 'Maybe I heard it from far away, the sound of the trumpet, for I did not live near the clock tower.'

'It's just a story, isn't it?'

'You think so?'

'It is, isn't it?' But he did not speak when she tugged his arm. 'Isn't it?'

The cup of his pipe flamed as he sucked deeply at the stem. When Seth, the man who owned the store, came in to show him a broken alarm clock, Joseph took the pipe out of his mouth and slowly pressed out the red glow.

Seth, a small quick man with pointed ears, winked at Anna and called her grandfather 'Joey'. After he took away the repaired watches, Joseph opened the back of the alarm clock and mumbled to it in words from the other side.

'You see,' he said to Anna, 'I never knew I was going to be a fixer of clocks, a watchmaker. No, my father told everyone I was studying to be a rabbi. And they believed him.'

There was so much happiness in the room, like a hot summer's day when the heat cast her down. In the place where her bed used to be, across the room from where her parents slept, stood a crib. Saul walked to the window holding a wrinkled doll he said was her brother Michael. Sylvia touched Anna around the shoulders and made sounds of encouragement to her son. She moved away from her daughter to Saul who handed her the baby. Anna watched as she rocked him slowly in her arms, then shifted him against her shoulder. He made a funny noise like a balloon losing air and her parents laughed. Anna tried to swallow, choked and coughed till her father tapped her sharply on the back. She put up her hands.

'Not yet Anna. When he's bigger you can hold him.' But she had not wanted to hold him; she was reaching to be picked up.

Sylvia put the baby in the crib and tucked a blanket around him and then they stood watching him. Anna would sleep in the living room now, nearer the sounds.

On the first night she lay on the sofa, the stone woman pulled at Anna till she fell to the floor with her blankets still around her. Saul came running when he heard crying. She was still asleep when he picked her up, but her mouth was moving.

The woman returned and returned. She danced through the night an angry dance. Promise you'll let me stay with you she said as her face hardened into stone.

Anna was listening to scenes in her head. Like books she read when one person began talking and then another answered and a third, a person not there, described what they were doing.

They were out beyond Anna's street, beyond even Jack's candy store and the Chinese laundry, walking under the overhead rails just as a train went by hailing sparks. Anna ran while her mother yelled, 'It won't hurt you.'

People left bits of themselves on the street: a bobby pin, a cigarette butt, a broken pearl necklace her mother said was not real. She must not pick up things from the ground for they might have polio germs, but she looked at them and sometimes when there was a string of ants she got down on her haunches to watch them working.

An orange caterpillar had wandered out from the safety of a patch of dusty grass across the white square of the sidewalk. It was while she was prodding its fur that Sylvia's flowered dress disappeared. She waited for her mother to appear, then ran up the wide road to an intersection where cars chased each other around a sidewalk island, but could not find her way back to the caterpillar who didn't want to crawl onto her hand and come away with her.

She knew the streets but not the secret to the puzzle of how to return home. Somewhere in the puzzle her mother moved and the grey stone of her building stood, the rooms where they woke and ate and shouted at each other.

She turned from the rush of cars down a shabby street with low brown buildings, stoops full of children she had never seen before. The street ended with the blind wall of a rumbling factory where a group of boys ran and hit a ball and yelled at her to get out of their way. Two small girls sitting one above the other on the steps leading up to one of the buildings stared at Anna as she walked back from the blind wall. They both wore house slippers and the older one was combing the hair of a rubber doll.

'I'm lost,' Anna said to them.

The younger girl asked, 'Don't you have a mother?'

106

'I do. But I can't find her.'

'You live around here?' the older girl asked.

'I live on Webster Avenue. Ten twenty four Webster Avenue,' she said to the uncomprehending faces of the little girls.

Someone was calling from inside; the older one took the younger by the hand and they turned their backs on Anna. The house slippers made a sound like paper against paper as they walked up the remaining stairs and into the building.

They're sisters, Anna thought. Why they left her without speaking.

Anna sat down on the step where the older sister had sat cradling her half-naked dolly. Her legs trembled from running and she could not hear her breathing. Sometimes at night after the lights went out in the apartment, after her parents' whispering had ceased, the stone woman lay on her chest till Anna gasped. 'Mommy,' she cried out, but as Sylvia brushed her hair back from her face, pulled the blankets up over her shoulders, she did not hear the breath going out of Anna's body and into the woman. Her chest squeezed like the black balloon the doctor pumped on the band around her mother's arm.

'Whoops!' A man stumbled on the stairs and seeing her face, asked 'What's the matter?'

He came closer, his blotchy face with the familiar smell like the doorway of the White Gander, a dark narrow room across from the Chinese laundry where men sat on stools and drank from large glasses.

'Where's your mommy?' He held on the bannister to keep himself from falling, but he was leaning towards her more and more.

As she ran down the street, she heard him cry after her, 'Hey, little girl. Hey, I won't hurt you. Why you wanna run away like that?'

Ahead she saw the black overhead rails of the train and recognized the long noisy street. She waited in front of Smiling Johnny's, the vegetable store where her mother bought real farm tomatoes, brown eggs and Indian nuts, for the frowning man to emerge. She had never noticed before how the train threw black dust on the piles of potatoes and carrots he kept outside. She thought if she waited long enough near the store, her mother's angry face would appear, but she was not among the silent faces which flowed down the street and under the rails.

Anna walked on, holding her ears against the sound of the train, till she came to the Palace movie theater where she had seen *Snow White and the Seven Dwarfs* and screamed at the stepmother's face. But it was a different movie they had on now and there were pictures of adults kissing in the glass cases. She leaned against the glass, then slid to the ground indifferent to the ticket seller who knocked against her window to get Anna's attention. People began to come out, each one pausing to adjust to the flash of the sun, to stare at the child who sat crumpled up on the sidewalk, her face stained with tears.

She ran from their stares, their words and followed an old man, small and sad like Grandpa Joseph, in a black hat, who left the Palace as if in a trance, wiping his eyes with the tassels of his shiny white scarf. When he turned the corner, she recognized the synagogue, the square yellow building which stood so near the rails of the train.

On the High Holy Days she stood at the back of the room with her father while the man at the front in long robes wailed and another spoke words she could not understand. When they entered, Grandma Brenner turned from chanting into her black book, from swaying and bowing in her place among the old women and men, to smile at her granddaughter. Anna and her father remained at the back because they had not bought tickets and should not be in the room at all.

They waited near an open patch of weeds in the sidewalk. Anna pulled at the tall dry golden stalks but they resisted and her hands soon showed the red marks of her struggle. Grandma Brenner came away from a group of women; small and stately, she crossed over to Anna and Saul. First she kissed Saul, then she pulled Anna into her arms and kissed her three times, once on the forehead and then on each cheek. Russian kisses she called her rough embraces.

'You'll come for schnapps?' Grandma Brenner always asked though they had known hours ago that they would stroll back with her to the two-room apartment with the plants grown from the cast-off seeds of lemons and oranges.

'For a sweet year.' They stood holding tiny thick glasses before a round table covered with a thin plastic tablecloth, grey with gaudy roses. Grandma Brenner cut Saul a slice of yellow sponge, Anna a piece of honey cake, and offered her a sip of brown liquor which stung her mouth and throat, made her feel the pain of sweetness, the birth of a year.

Now as the old man mounted the steps to the synagogue, Anna stood watching, hoping he would turn and beckon to her. Then she could go in and sit with her grandma. But he disappeared into the yellow building without even noticing her. She waited by the patch of weeds for Grandma Brenner to emerge, to walk slowly across the street as if in time to some inner music. But no one came out so she crossed over, sat down on the steps and listened to the low murmurs of the old people praying. A train roared in and when it left, revealed a lone voice singing.

On the dazzling white steps a figure in dark clothes came towards Anna. The woman from the basement, the witch.

'Is your mother in there?' She crouched over Anna, then touched the wetness under her eyes. 'What happened to make you cry?'

'I did not see your mother in there.' She spoke half to herself, half to Anna.

'Lost,' Anna whispered, 'I'm lost.'

'But you're so close to home.' She held out her hand. 'Come.'

Anna stood up but did not take her hand.

'Come. Take my hand. We have big streets to cross before we come home.'

Her face was heart-shaped, her large close-set eyes regarded Anna with a seriousness she had never known. On her heavy dark green suit she wore a pin of gleaming jewels, red and purple fruit which hung on twisted stems of gold. The colors whirled before Anna's eyes until the woman moved out of the sun and the pin became a piece of metal with glass stones. She was hot and wiped her face with a small flowered handkerchief, the kind Anna had seen tucked in the compartments of Grandma Brenner's pocketbook when she opened it to give Anna a choice of peanuts or hard candies.

'Why are you afraid of me, you and your friend? I hear you.'

Anna could hardly understand her words through the thickness of her speech.

'Do you think I am a bad woman?'

'Are you a witch?'

'What do you think?' But she did not wait for an answer. 'They have no witches here, no, but I have known ones before I came over.'

They began walking down Webster Avenue. 'What makes you think this? You know I had two daughters, not so different from you.'

'Where are they?'

She did not answer and then she said 'Look. There's your mother with a policeman. How you have worried her.'

Sylvia ran forward leaving the policeman standing beside the baby carriage.

'Two hours she was lost,' she told the woman. Then turning to Anna, 'You let go of me. Never again, you hear? You'll hold on to me from now on.'

The woman from the basement was called Doris Wasserman, and she sat for the first time at their kitchen table sucking her tea through a cube of sugar.

'Your daughter thinks I'm a witch.'

'Anna, that's not nice,' Sylvia said to the girl who was wandering about the room with a glass of chocolate milk.

'She's impossible.' Sylvia shook her fist at Anna. 'Did you know that Mrs Wasserman used to paint pictures?'

'But that was before the war.' Doris Wasserman held up her hands as if to show the absence of a paintbrush. 'I have no more

pictures in me. Now I'm learning to type.'
'You'll show us your pictures some time,' said Sylvia.
'They're gone. No. One must be realistic.'
'But you'll start again. You must.'
'No, it's finished. And I was never so good. Not like the others, my friends.'
Anna walked away from the two women and lay on the sofa, her bed at night. As she closed her eyes she heard Doris say to her mother, 'Let her sleep, she must be tired from walking.'
Her mother said, 'Poor tyke.'
She woke once to the sound of their murmuring voices, and then she was running down a street towards her mother who walked with her head bowed. However fast Anna ran she could not catch up with her and then her mother disappeared leaving her in a narrow corridor, her chest burning with the colors of Mrs Wasserman's pin which she could not remove.
When she woke, Doris Wasserman had left. Sounds which were not words came from the table in the kitchen. Sylvia's face was ugly, petulant like a baby's.
'Stop it.' Anna pulled at her mother's hand which she had raised to her mouth to cover her sobs.
Sylvia began to rub her eyes, back and forth, roughly, the way she wiped stains from her daughter's face.
'She lost her children, her little girls.'
'But can't she find them?' Anna looked at her mother's exhausted face. 'Can't she?'
'Don't bother me.' Sylvia stood up, went to the refrigerator, pulled out a bowl of raw chicken. Anna followed her with her mouth formed in another question. 'You're in my way,' Sylvia said before she could speak.

On Saturday afternoon when her parents went away, Anna stayed with Doris Wasserman, the first time she had descended to the apartment beneath the building. Her parents took the baby but told her she was too young to come.
Doris's apartment was even smaller than Grandma Brenner's, and no light found its way through the small square

111

windows. But Doris had painted the walls white, hung up large colored pictures from magazines of mountains and prairies, and prints in which bright shapes whirled and clashed. The day was warm but Doris wore a long-sleeved blue dress; her soft heart-shaped face was pale with the heat.

'Why couldn't I go with them?' Anna complained.

'A hospital is not a place for a little girl.'

They had not told her that; all her mother said was that they were visiting friends.

'Why are they going there?'

'Haven't they told you? They're visiting your grandmother, your mother's mother. She's sick.'

'What's wrong with her?'

'She... her head is bothering her.'

Anna had not seen Tamar for nearly a year, not since the baby came. Nobody said why they never went there anymore for tea and Anna had to think hard to remember her grandmother's face.

One afternoon they had visited Grandpa Joseph in his shop and went for lemon tea and cake to the delicatessen across the street. Before they parted Joseph slipped something cool and smooth into Anna's palm.

'What was that?' Sylvia asked for she had seen the movement between the old man and her daughter. When Anna showed her the narrow lady's watch with its tarnished band, its old-fashioned face, she said, 'It's broken. Typical.'

Anna closed her fingers tightly over the watch and would not open her fist again to her mother.

It became a princess, the watch; she tied bits of toilet paper around its face for hair and gave it rides in the ceramic compartments of the lazy susan.

Doris returned from the kitchen with two plates of steaming green bundles. Anna pierced one with her fork and discovered hamburger meat.

'Have you never had?' Doris asked. 'Try it. Just a little piece.' She cut off a section of the green bundle. Anna put it in her mouth, sucked at it for a moment, the way Michael did when offered pieces of chicken for the first time. It tasted both rancid and sweet, like the grass she once pulled up and chewed in Bronx Park.

Doris watched her eating the stuffed cabbage, not an intrusive stare like those from the men and women who sat from morning till dusk on benches in the park, but a look which meant that she too chewed the foreign green leaves, felt the pungency against her tongue, she too had difficulty swallowing the heavy meat. Sometimes her mouth moved slightly as if mimicking Anna's, like Sylvia's when she spooned the smooth orange baby food past Michael's lips, as if by moving her mouth she could help him eat.

'You've done well,' Doris said when Anna told her she could not finish.

She brought the dishes into her tiny kitchen and returned with shiny brown cake topped with almonds, a glass of yellow tea for herself, one of milk for Anna. As Doris sipped, Anna remembered the wrinkled skin of Tamar's mouth, her smile which was not a smile, and a pain like a fist squeezing her stomach pushed out the words 'Grandma's a witch.'

'No, no. She's just not feeling well. If you knew what she's been through.'

'What's the matter with her?'

'In the old days they would say another soul entered her, making her do strange things, but now they say she's unhappy. You see? She's very, very sad and sometimes when old people are sad they need to rest.'

Doris put an end to her words by getting up from the table. Anna's stomach was churning. She did not want to talk anymore about Tamar but there was something she did not know, something she could not get at, like a splinter gone deep under her skin.

Anna brought her empty glass and plate into the narrow little kitchen. Doris stood at the sink, her back to Anna, her sleeves rolled up, her hands moving under the running water. On Doris's pale soft arm Anna saw dark marks like figures from a book. She moved closer, reached out to touch them.

113

Doris turned and tried to pull down the sleeve but Anna had already seen the numbers.

'Go. Go away.'

Anna ran from the hot room, from the smell of cabbage, gas, the perfumed sweat which rose from Doris's body. She ran because what was inside her could no longer be held back, and at the entrance to the bathroom she vomited a heavy liquid. Again and again till her throat burned and her body wavered before the black and white tiled floor.

Doris was holding her forehead and saying something about new food and heat. 'Is it all out?' she asked.

She noticed after Doris put her to bed that she had pulled down the sleeves of her dress.

'Sleep,' Doris whispered, but Anna was tugging at her sleeve even as her eyes were shutting.

'Why?' Anna mumbled.

'Because you've been sick.'

'No I mean.' Again she tugged at the sleeve, but Doris drew back beyond her grasp. She pulled the curtains across the twilight windows and the room went black.

I have kept the photograph though it is badly faded with age, the brilliant colors gone yellow and brown, but our expressions remain as clear as when we were four. We stood at separate easels, paintbrushes poised over large empty sheets of paper, both of us naked to the waist with the protruding stomachs of infants, our faces turned towards the camera. She was not smiling, no, even then her pale chubby face was grave.

Our parents were part of a circle of friends, and for a time Susan and I saw each other at bungalow colonies up in the Catskills and brunches in apartments around the Bronx. Our history is what united us as we grew rapidly apart, our history and the photograph which sat on my parents' dresser framing our innocence.

When Susan was seven, her family moved to a house out in Long Island. For years we did not see each other but our parents kept in touch by telephone. Susan had become a gifted child. She could speak French and play the piano. I did not know how I was reported by my parents, nor did I care much.

I had just turned fourteen when I saw Susan again. I was surprised how little she had changed; still small, round-faced, she had the body of a child. Probably she wears an undershirt I thought and felt superior. Our parents brought us together again out of desperation, for we had both entered our teens with the stigma of intellectual upon us. But this I did not guess until later. At the time it seemed a natural enough reunion.

Odd things she remembered about our summers together, but she looked blank when I mentioned the easel and our art. A grasshopper with one leg who came to her secret place, hadn't she shown me it? The lake whose surface I broke with thrusts of my arms and legs while my father held me, the lake had creatures which frightened her: orange salamanders, tiny blue fish. I only remember the muddy water, the hairy chests of the men, the raft which I never reached.

'And the storms. So many. Once we stood under a tree with

our parents, yes you were there, yes, because you cried.' She
looked at me as if to fix her memory in my mind. It was one of
the few moments she ever noticed me.

'You cried when you saw the lightning.'

'And you, didn't you cry?'

Susan shook her head in her solemn, baby-faced way I
would find so exasperating. 'It was beautiful. And a man died.
He'd been swimming in the lake when the storm began. He
laughed when they shouted at him to come back. He said, "I
like to swim by lightning".'

'I don't remember anything like that. A man dying. I
wouldn't forget that. Who was he?'

'Nobody even knew his name. They didn't want me to know
but I crept out of the cabin after all the grown-ups went down
to the lake and crawled through the high grass so they couldn't
see me. When they pulled him out, his body was covered with
shining black mud, but I saw the mark of the lightning.'

'C'mon. What could you see?'

'You think I'm making it up?'

'You know when you're little you imagine things and then
they become real.'

'But I'll never forget. The red scar across his stomach. And
I ran away when I saw it. And I would never go into the lake
again.'

That I remembered, how Susan cried when her mother
brought her near the water. She never learned to swim.

Susan rarely talked about her family, but I remembered them.
They did not look like her. Her older sister was dark, slender,
angular, her parents small and trim with narrow mocking eyes.
Her father, a lawyer, liked to utter sharp little comments which
everyone found witty. Sometimes I thought Susan had been
adopted, that her parents hadn't told her the truth. I wondered if
she was made of the same stuff as I was; if I pinched her would
she cry out? This is what fascinated me at the beginning.

We met at the Metropolitan Museum of Art, in the great
dark halls of the Egyptian wing. It was there in the shadows of
the Pharaohs caught with one foot in front of the other that she

first told me of the pains.

'Mummies.'

'What?'

She was bent over, her hand clutching at her belly. 'I've got the mummies.'

We rushed to the bathroom where I waited, watching her feet stir beneath the stall door. Once the cramps disappeared, Susan seemed to forget she'd ever had them and ignored my sympathetic remarks. She had been too excited, that was all.

But some time after we returned to the Pharaohs, her chubby face reddened, like a baby ready to open her bowels.

'I'm getting them again,' she whispered.

'The mummies?'

She nodded. I wanted to laugh, but I thought, suppose she dies?

Something inside her grew too fast in the presence of beauty, in my presence; something beat against the walls of her stomach, ran hotly through her and she must rid herself of it over and over again. What it was I did not understand, but I knew enough not to tell my parents of her pain.

In the summer the museum was a cool dead place; we rarely saw anyone but the guards as we strolled through the Greek and Roman rooms, past Demeter and a headless Zeus. Susan always wanted to return to the Pharaohs. I found them stiff and unfeeling, but she said they had style, they had control.

But we hardly looked at the statues. We thought separately about our separate lives. We exchanged monologues about school: the boys we pretended to hate, the teachers we feared and loved, the politics we learned from our parents but claimed as our own. I would speak and then Susan; there was never any exchange.

I knew she looked forward to walking with me through these silent halls, that she initiated these meetings. As if afraid of losing me, Susan allowed me to lead, to decide which rooms in the museum we would visit first, to talk more than she did. Yet she could not have been more indifferent. When we parted at the subway, I felt lonely, not from the sudden separation from a friend, but from a day with a stranger I knew.

During that year we went to the Museum of Modern Art, to the Whitney and once to a large white gallery on Park Avenue. It was never enough to meet, just meet without a plan; we needed a destination, some point beyond ourselves on which to converge.

I was growing, losing what my mother called my baby fat, and I had begun to wear a bra, while Susan remained small, unformed. We were both waiting with an anxiety we dared not admit for the moment girls at school boasted about. I know now that we feared becoming the odd one of the two of us, the one who hadn't started, the one left out of the blessing.

I began to be ashamed of her, to dread meeting those friends I made in junior high school. But I was relieved too; at least I did not look like her and knew enough not to wear a wool kerchief around my head and my glasses in public. Not that Susan was ugly; with her large eyes, her soft, unblemished skin, she could have been as pretty as she had been as a child at the easel. But her expression did not invite cuddling.

Susan wanted to become a composer. While I listened to Beatles songs, she learned to play fugues and sonatas. She talked about Bach and Mozart as if they lived with her. Sometimes when we walked through Central Park, she sang in a high trembly voice tunes I could not identify. I knew I could not tell her to stop, that I had no cause to hate her singing, so I remained silent till we left the Park.

She continued to have 'the mummies'. After our lunch she would rush to the bathroom. I did not follow her anymore for I knew she would emerge after some time looking normal.

Only once did we pass a day together when she did not have pain in her belly. We were eating lunch at a coffee shop near the Museum of Modern Art. Susan always had a salad sandwich, just lettuce and tomato between soft white bread, and a milky drink, while I ate hamburgers and French fries. She scorned my choices as she did the menus of these places; they did not have the food she wanted, but she could not say what this was.

The waitress came towards us balancing a tray with plates of our food, my Coke and Susan's malted milkshake. I remember the waitress smiled at me, perhaps because I was the only one who looked up at her in room of heads bent over food or menus. Suddenly she turned pale, the smile gone from her face. The tray slipped from her hands as she fell and began to writhe on the floor. The manager rushed over and tried to put a spoon between her teeth. Another waitress came and hovered over the woman, calling her name over and over until the manager told her to go away. At the far end of the room, people stood up to see what was happening. Susan watched as if from behind a glass case at the museum.

And then it ended. The waitress stood up, embarrassed, apologetic, despairing. The manager sent her home and took over her tables. I heard him say to a customer: 'I never knew. If she had told me. She should've you know.'

A man in a dirty apron swept up the broken glass and the food which never reached us. The manager brought us new drinks, another salad sandwich, my hamburger, but I could not eat.

'What's gonna happen to her? She'll get fired for sure,' I said.

Susan took a large bite of her sandwich. The sight of the white bread disappearing into her mouth made me sick to my stomach.

'She got up pretty fast. Like it was nothing,' she said.

'What do you mean? I thought she was going to die.'

'You couldn't see. I saw everything.'

'I saw.' But I could not go on without crying in front of her.

Susan finished her sandwich, was sucking up the remains of her milkshake through a straw. I could see she was waiting for me to change the subject, but I kept silent.

'What's your favorite Beethoven symphony?' she asked, only to give her own answer. She knew how ignorant I was of such music.

When I shrugged, she said 'Mine's the Pastoral.' Her enthusiasm had a hardness about it which upset me. But I was certain that after we returned to the museum, she would spend

119

an hour in one of the stalls of the bathroom paying for her pleasure.

But she had no pains that day. She walked back and forth in front of Picasso's *Guernica*. She seemed to smile at the jigsaw of screaming faces. I turned away from her euphoria, told her I wasn't feeling well and had to leave early.

I will never remember if we chose to meet on the day of the solar eclipse or if it was just our luck. When I climbed up from the subway, I noticed that the sky had already lost much of its light.

Susan was standing on the steps of the Metropolitan Museum holding two pieces of cardboard. 'Don't look up,' she said, 'you'll go blind. We'll watch it through here.'

I sat down on the steps clutching my knees. I had a dull ache in my belly, but she didn't notice.

'Can we wait till the sun's completely covered before we go in?' she begged me like a child. I wondered why it excited her so much to look at light and shadows moving across a piece of cardboard.

'I don't care,' I said.

People stood on the steep steps leading up to the museum holding pieces of wood or cardboard, their eyes averted from the dark sun. I noticed that Susan had her head lowered even when she talked to me, but she saw the man standing on the top step looking straight up at the sky with his hands cupped around his eyes. A woman told him not to look up, but he ignored her.

I thought he looked peculiar, but not like the people I shunned on the subway. Everything he wore was a luminous blue: bell bottom pants, embroidered shirt, headband, even his shoes, and on his hands silver rings with large turquoise stones. His face was older than the rest of him: lean cheeks with deep wrinkles like scars, a face tense with smiling. From time to time he would shake his fingers and make his knuckles crack, laugh and slap his thigh.

The others on the steps smirked at each other when they saw this, but Susan's face was grim. 'He'll go blind,' she said each time he made a movement of delight. I could see it was difficult for her to concentrate on her vision of the eclipse. 'He will, you know. I'm sure of it.' She wanted me to agree; for once my opinion was important to her.

'You don't know for sure,' I said.

'He hasn't stopped staring up there. He'll go blind. Definitely.' With that she found her concentration again.

It was dark now like a sudden storm without wind, rain or lightning. The turquoise man was performing a little dance, chanting in some language I had never heard before.

'Lunatic,' someone whispered.

The people on the steps began to go into the museum, but Susan continued to stare down at her piece of cardboard.

'Let's go in,' I said for I was bored and my body felt swollen and tender.

Susan began to hum a tune. Probably it was from some opera, but I could not be sure. It was not humming exactly, not singing either, more like the trilling of a bird. The sounds emerged from her throat; her lips did not move.

The turquoise man grew silent, his hands fell to his sides, his face grew solemn in the strange light. 'Shush,' he whispered. Perhaps she did not hear him for the sounds from her throat were louder than his admonition.

I watched the two of them, wondering whose will would be stronger; she perched like a small plump bird on the stone step, he a wild gaudy creature landed by freak chance in the middle of the city.

He put his hands over his ears and swayed back and forth as if to some hidden music. Then he looked at her, at the trilling which would not stop. Suddenly he rushed down the stairs, so fast that we felt the wind of his flight.

She said, 'When he goes blind, he'll regret it.'

'At least he saw the eclipse,' I said.

'I saw. I did. I had it all here.' She cupped her hands.

'All you saw were shadows.'

'But I understood it.'

She still had her hands cupped when I said, 'I gotta go in.' I ran up the steps of the museum not caring if Susan followed me.

I went straight to the bathroom without her, for once without her. The blood had soaked through to my jeans.

She looked like a little kid standing outside. 'You didn't have to wait,' I said, 'I'm going home anyway.'

She nodded as if she knew. Maybe she'd seen the stains and not told me.

'I started,' I whispered.

She didn't say anything to this.

'And I got bad cramps.' It wasn't true.

'Do you think you'll always have them?' she asked.

'I don't know. I hope not.'

'Because I won't,' Susan said. She turned and made her way to the Egyptians.

When the stars threw down their spears,
And water'd heaven with their tears,
Did he smile his work to see?
Did he who made the Lamb make thee?

William Blake, 'The Tyger'

By the time he was seventeen, John Lasky called himself a Nazi. He kept a knife in a secret place close to his heart, wore a belt whose buckle was inlaid with a swastika and chased the young boys coming home from Hebrew school down the streets of the Bronx.

But he had been a frightened little boy himself. When his teacher dragged him up to the front of the room to recite the poems he wrote about monsters and warrior kings, he tried to turn away from the children who repulsed him, but she held him fast. With his drawn face, the shadows of insomnia under his eyes and his stooped figure, he looked like a miniature of his father.

When John turned nine and began writing sonnets, his father had become a gaunt old man who sat alone in his black hat and coat on a park bench. He sidled away from his wife as she moved through their narrow apartment calling her son. She had always looked after family, had pulled the bullies off her little brothers and coaxed words from her father after a stroke paralysed his mouth. She was Protestant, a cheerful Calvinist who met her husband while working for a Christian refugee organization after the war. He had come from a displaced persons' camp, a Polish Jew who could not say where he had been or where his mother lay. John was christened and confirmed, for the father would not enter a synagogue. Once he said: 'I am not speaking to God.' John could never devour the blood and flesh of the maimed godson without choking.

John made up games he could play by himself, and read the volumes of Dickens, Twain and Kipling which his father kept on a shelf above the television. His father had been a history professor but lost his job during the 1950s when the chairman of his department accused him of being sympathetic to the Russian Revolution. When asked to deny this, he remained silent; he was habitually silent, but the chairman was happy to take this as guilt. He needed to purge someone.

The family moved up to the Bronx and survived on the wife's salary as a substitute teacher, for the father could not bring himself to search for work. It was not indolence or pride but a lassitude which settled over him, staying his hand when he reached for the telephone and so confusing him that he could not decide which direction to walk when he left the house. John was bathed and fed by his father whose hands were never gentle. His indifference, the mask of bitterness, terrified the boy, who thought he might be left to starve by the old man.

John was happiest when they went to the park together, the father reading a book while the boy dug a hole in the earth which would take him all the way to China. They'd return home in the late afternoon, the father to sit idly in the living room, the little boy to his solitary play. The apartment was quiet until the mother returned with bags of food and stories about her students. As she talked her husband went into the bedroom to lie down, and the boy was left to listen.

Once John rose in the night and seeing a light under the living room door, he entered. His father sat with his robe wrapped tightly around him staring silently at his books.

'Go back to sleep,' he said.

'What's wrong?' asked the boy.

But the father did not answer. The boy stood there for some time watching the white profile, waiting for the mouth to open again.

Then the father heard a sound from his son, the first time he heard him cry since he was a baby.

'What's the matter?' He turned to look at John. 'Eh? What is it? A bad dream?'

'You,' John sobbed.

He was bullied for a time in school, but the other boys feared his stare; they could not even pity him when he stuttered, for he rejected anyone who offered kindness. The teachers described him as a nervous child, his body quivering at the slightest touch. When he volunteered to answer a question, he would only half stand, his voice a whisper.

Only his mother could touch him, for she let him know that he was better than the others, the boys who pushed him aside in the schoolyard, the smart alecks who shouted out the answers to the multiplication drill, the fully Jewish boys who recited litanies in a strange guttural tongue to each other. He would be a great man some day, would laugh at the boys he feared, laugh at himself for having feared. He was chosen and, like the enchanted hero, would emerge from his stooped frame a god.

He grew tall, lanky, but his face never seemed to change from the watchful eyes, the dead white skin, the trembling mouth. He began to wander the streets alone at night, telling his mother he was going to the library. He walked through empty playgrounds, stared into the dark windows of a toyshop with his shoulders hunched, his head turning from one side to other. If he saw someone who knew him he crossed the street or ducked into the doorway of one of the apartment buildings. He was establishing his own territory; no one could enter his night world, not even his mother.

Once he stayed out later than usual and, coming down his street, he met his father who had gone out to look for him. The old man stood before his son, his white scarf shining in the lamplight.

'Where do you go?'

The boy tried to walk past, but his father blocked him. 'I asked you something.'

'Nowhere. I just walk around.'

The father appeared to smile. 'Your mother was worried,' he said, implying that he was not. 'You won't go out again at night without telling us where?'

John nodded. He was not a natural rebel; he wanted only to

be left alone.

He turned instead to model building. He was a meticulous worker. With his long thin fingers like tapers he built Spitfires and Mosquitoes, helicopters and submarines. He staged battles in his room, the bombers drawing closer and closer to the cities he created from toy soldiers and blocks. His thin voice imitated their sounds with a kind of shriek, and then came the explosions from a mouth which could never shape the words he wanted. When it was over he was sweating, but he smiled to see his work: the towers destroyed, the toy soldiers scattered across the wooden floor.

Once his mother entered the room but his back was to the door, so he did not see and through his battle sounds could not hear her. She saw him touching himself as he played and reached over to pull his hand out of his pants. He was crying but, when she tried to take him in her arms, he shook her off; they were tears of outrage, not sorrow, and she began to think that she had borne an abnormal child, not an exceptional one.

Bruce Stein was so voluble that he spat when he talked. Black-haired with the smile of a wily baby, he had all the anarchy of genius and the strength of a young Titan. In kindergarten he threw blocks at the other children and tried to rip the roof off the playhouse. By third grade he had been tamed into performing scientific experiments, but the teacher knew that she could never turn her back on him. When the other bright children were allowed to skip a year, Bruce was held back by the principal because she thought him immature.

His mother wondered where he had come from, this large violent baby who drank from her veins, it seemed. Her husband was a squat, quiet man who laboured in an engineering firm, and she had wanted nothing more than to wheel her carriage in the park with the other women, inclining her head to hear their gossip. But Bruce did not like to sleep and his crying form seemed to explode in the carriage; when she rocked him as she saw the other mothers do, she felt absurd.

He was respectful of his mother, almost protective of her

as he grew older, but was not mindful of her admonitions to stop bullying the other children. Sometimes he had allies, boys who would crouch with him behind the bushes outside the playground, spring at the groups of girls emerging with their jump rope and demand a payment of a penny each for the privilege of continuing on their way unaccosted. But the allies never became friends, for Bruce was willing to turn against them if he had the chance. He had no loyalties except to his mother. On the day she told him about the principal's decision, she saw his proud head droop for the first time. All his life he had surged forward and now it was as if he saw the limits of his mortality.

When Bruce met John Lasky one evening at the library, they were both fifteen but a grade apart, for John had been deemed mature enough to skip a year in junior high school. Though they had been in the same classes together in elementary school, they had hardly ever spoken. Bruce did not bully the weak, there was no challenge in it, so he had left the stuttering boy alone.

John had begun to read far beyond the level of the books in his high school. While his English teacher was intent on *Of Mice and Men*, John was returning from the library with *War and Peace* and *The Iliad*. He was almost happy as he lost himself in these vast stories, yet when he finished each one, he felt dissatisfied. The questions he read into the opening chapters were never answered, or if they were, he suspected that the authors did not truly believe what they said.

He turned instead to the truths of Plato, Nietzsche and Marx. Ignorant of the history which produced these thinkers, and without the guidance of a teacher or the softening influence of discussion, he drew certain simple conclusions. He believed in perfection, this was what was meant by God; flawless models of humankind, like the robots he saw on *Twilight Zone*, existed somewhere beyond the infected men and women he drew away from.

His teachers knew nothing of his reading. They hardly noticed the quiet boy who gave them no trouble, whose papers were immaculate. When his mother went to see his teachers,

127

they had to think hard to remember him, stopping themselves just in time from saying, 'Oh, you mean the one with the stutter.'

John was silent, yet he struggled to contain his thoughts; he imagined battalions marching down the convolutions of his brain; sometimes he wondered if the others could hear the orders he gave, the thunder of their boots, the cries of exaltation.

At fifteen John was just a taller version of his boyhood self, but Bruce had lost control over his body. His voice broke early. He became burly and sweated even in winter, so that his mother found him in the morning moist and naked with the covers twisted like swaddling around him. He became shy before her and waited until she was gone from the house before he satisfied the lust which never seemed to leave him, but grew with each feeding like a tapeworm inside him.

He had been thrown out of the children's room of the library because he liked to read his favorite stories out loud, and once during the fairy tale hour he pulled the book from the librarian. She was reading too slowly, he told his mother. When he was thirteen the librarian relented, gave him an adult card, and led him to the teenage section. Soon he was carrying home Victor Hugo, Dickens, Balzac, the weighty novels like large building blocks in his arms. But it was the great sagas of history which he loved: the bloody court intrigues, the ancient battles, the facts which he could memorize and hold like talismans against the uncertainties of his life.

When John did not emerge from his cocoon in high school as his mother had hoped, she decided to send him to a psychiatric clinic in Manhattan which had a sliding scale of fees. She was worried not only by his silence and the worsening of his stutter, but by his lack of friends.

'He doesn't talk to anybody,' she told her husband. 'It's not normal.'

'But he's always been that way,' he said.

'I thought he'd grow out of it.'

'What's "it"?'

'Don't make fun of me.'

He became frail before his wife's belligerence and so tired

he felt like he was drowning as he lay on the soft old sofa. He thought in a few years his son would leave home, and then he could regain his wits.

'He's your child,' she said. More and more this was what she believed, that her son had been cast from the brain of her husband.

Dr Goldwitz specialized in teenagers. She was a short, broad-shouldered woman with straight brown hair and bangs which ended just above her glasses. When John could not produce an early childhood memory, she asked him how he felt about being there. He had almost a physical reaction to her, to her brittle smile and the soft hand she extended when they met.

She continued to probe him with questions, alternating the bland with the significant to catch him out: 'What do you do after school? Do you meet friends? Girlfriends? Don't you have a girlfriend? Do you think your mother wants you to have one? Is that a good book? Tell me about it in your own words? Can't you tell me? Why, what is it about being here with me?' She was always bringing herself into his life; this was what he could not abide. In one session she tried to match his silence, but the air in the still room filled with his poison and choked her. She had to speak.

By the fourth session she grew impatient, her demeanour no longer distant and slightly mysterious, her questions edged with anger. She said they would play a game. He would tell her the first thing that came to his mind. When he did not speak, she said she wondered if he was thinking about her. He shook his head.

'Then about your parents? Your father perhaps? What's he doing right now?'

'I don't know.'

'Is he working?' She knew he was not.

'He doesn't have a job.'

'So what does he do?'

'Lies in bed.'

'All day?'

'Yes, all day he lies in bed, then he gets up to eat, then he lies down again.'

They grew silent over the image of the prone father. Then she asked: 'Every day he does that? Doesn't he go out?'

'No, he just lies there.'

John clutched the arms of the chair to keep from screaming at her.

It was not enough now to wander out past the elevated subway to the treeless avenues of bars and hardware stores, to stand on the bridge with a wasteland at his back watching the cars stream out of the city. Bruce felt as if he had been imprisoned in a tiny cell all his life, bound by the barren streets, the classrooms where the chairs pressed his body, the other children like flimsy dolls.

He began to go downtown on Saturday mornings, at first to the places his mother had taken him, Central Park Zoo and the hot dog stands in Times Square, but soon he was leaving the subway at unfamiliar stations, staying on buses until the end of their route in Harlem, the Bowery, the West Side docks. Bruce took the pieces of paper men thrust at him on street corners and followed demonstrations by running along the sidewalk. A Negro man handed him a newspaper and then chased him down the street demanding money. When Bruce refused, there was suddenly a group around him, a wall of dark, hard bodies. He had never been bullied before and now they pushed him to and fro, their fists like iron maces on his flesh. He tried to escape and was beaten to the ground.

Once he picked up a sign someone dropped in the street and ran to join the marchers. It was as if he had been thrust onto a moving stage. They shouted and sang 'He's got the whole world in his hands' as they strode all the way down Fifth Avenue to a rally in Washington Square.

That evening he felt calm and could sit at the dinner table without rocking in his chair or banging his spoon against the purple tin glass. His mother put her hand on his forehead and asked, 'Do you think you're coming down with something?'

Someone had taken an interest in him on the march, a skinny man with twisted grey hair, the face of an elf and the voice of a pedant. Harry belonged to the Peace Partisans, a group founded by men who had volunteered to fight Franco. Didn't Bruce see the connection with Vietnam? He did, but he was more impressed by the fact that they were real war heroes. Harry urged him to join their youth group, the Young Partisans, and wrote the address of the next meeting on the back of a leaflet showing a prone Negro man and the words, 'Fascism strikes home'.

The Young Partisans, most of them the sons and daughters of veterans of the movement, met in each other's apartments. Bruce was disappointed by the orderly square modern rooms, so like the ones he shared with his parents.

Bruce sat on the floor between a sour-faced boy in a leather jacket, and a girl who kept shaking back her long frizzy hair.

'Who brought you here?' the boy asked.

'Nobody.'

'Probably CIA.'

'Shut up, Chuck,' the girl said, then she turned to Bruce: 'Ignore him. He thinks he's Bob Dylan.'

A woman brought out potato chips and Cokes and asked him where he lived, who his parents were. 'Does your mother know you're here?'

He shook his head and smiled his baby smile. She brushed his cheek with the back of her hand in a way that made the hairs on his neck rise. 'You better tell her, honey,' she said.

Harry was talking about fresh blood, for theirs was already tired. They must all bring back one new friend, a possible convert. That was their assignment. Bruce grew restless in his chair, bored by the meeting's lack of firm purpose, by the side discussions which went on around him.

'Only one?' he called out, and everyone laughed.

He left when Harry stopped speaking and the young people turned to each other to talk of ordinary things.

He had noticed John Lasky before in the library. With his hunched shoulders, his arms darting towards the books, he had the furtive air of a thief. The two boys moved before the shelves, silent until Bruce turned to John: 'You ever read this?' He had a copy of *The Rise and Fall of the Third Reich.*

John Lasky shook his head and stared back at the shelves.

'Take it. I read it already.'

John hesitated, thinking that if he accepted the book he would have to continue talking to Bruce, but the boy was insistent.

'I'm reading Hermann Hesse. Haven't you read him? You should.' Bruce advanced towards John as he spoke, spitting, waving his hands at him. 'He's got this book about a man who becomes a wolf. Well, not really. It's dynamite.'

John found his voice. 'I don't like novels.'

'So what do you read?'

'History books.'

Bruce nodded. He felt he might have a convert or at least someone he could bring along to the meeting to show he had done his homework. For John could have no friends, no one to be with on Saturday afternoons when the meetings were held. He paused to stare at the boy, wondering how he could cajole him into coming. If he threatened him, John might confess it at the meeting or escape through the crowds as they left the subway.

John did not like to be so near Bruce; he thought he might choke from the boy's smell, but he was afraid to leave, afraid that if he showed his fear he might never escape. He turned back to the shelves and, as he pretended to read the titles of the books, he moved slowly away from Bruce, who continued to speak and gesticulate, his voice the loudest sound in the library.

The librarian, a rotund woman with full skirts, advanced towards them, her glasses swaying on a chain across her chest, her fingers to her lips. But Bruce had his back to her and when she tapped him, he spun around with a laugh which showed he thought her ludicrous.

He shouted goodbye to John as the librarian led him away and then stood guard over the flight of stairs which led to the street. It was only when he was outside that he realized the consequences; he was without books and might starve before she would let him in again, and he had missed his chance to win a convert.

But Bruce discovered that no one brought new people. Harry continued to urge them in his soft whine, but the Young Partisans remained a small group of teenagers who lounged on the floor playing gin rummy and chess, and necked in the empty bedrooms of their host.

Bruce forgot about John until he saw him on the subway one Saturday as he was on his way to an anti-war demonstration. Bruce carried his own banner, one of his mother's discarded sheets which he had painted with the words 'End the American Empire'. It was not an original slogan, but he felt as he painted it that the words could have been written at any time and would still be true when he was a grown man.

'Why don't you come? We're meeting in Central Park.'

'I got a dentist appointment.' It was what his mother had told him to say, so no one would know he was seeing a psychiatrist.

'So come afterwards.' Bruce grasped the boy's arm.

'I can't.'

'I'll meet you there. Where's the appointment?'

John shook his head but the boy's grasp was strong. He wondered what Dr Goldwitz would think if he didn't turn up. She would say he was avoiding her; she would make something of it.

John stared at the floor. The boy held him captive on the crowded train. He tried to make his body turn to stone, as he always did, but Bruce's hand sent the blood rushing from his arm to his face and made him tremble in spite of himself.

As the train approached his stop, John tried to break away, but Bruce held him fast. 'Then next time?'

John couldn't speak. Bruce said, 'I'll come get you.'

John nodded and Bruce let him go. 'Remember, I know where you live.'

Dr Goldwitz had told his mother they were finally getting somewhere. The boy showed his anger; he even raised his voice when her questioning grew persistent.

John knew that if he allowed her to break into him he would never be perfect again. He began to take out books by Freud. He memorized case histories and fed her the dreams of others. When she told him to stop playing games, he offered the stories of heroes from Greek mythology and dwelled on the rape scene in the epic of Gilgamesh. He thought she grew smaller with each session and imagined her disappearing entirely, leaving her oversize suit on her analyst's chair.

His mother, seeing no improvement in him, grew impatient with the cure which was costing her ten dollars a session. 'She hasn't helped him. To tell you the truth, he's worse,' she complained to the head of the clinic.

'How do you mean?'

'More silent. I think he's depressed.'

'Ah. That's often a sign that the therapy is working. These things take time.' The head of the clinic patted her shoulder.

But she was not fooled; he would continue to make excuses while he took her money and the creepy woman drained her son of what little life he possessed. She withdrew John from the clinic, and he enjoyed for the first time the taste of enemy blood.

Bruce appeared one Saturday morning when John was still in his pyjamas reading. 'Come on. Get dressed,' his mother pleaded. No one had ever come calling for her son before. When John said that he didn't want to go out, she crouched over him, whispering that Bruce would be hurt. Couldn't he go just this once? She had longed for him to have friends. She moved back and forth between the two boys, the one huddled in the darkened bedroom, the other standing in the tiny foyer smiling.

When the two boys emerged from the cool dark hall of the apartment building into the sun, Bruce said, 'We're meeting down at City Hall. You wanna come?'

John began to make excuses in his high stuttering voice.

'I told them you were coming.'

John shook his head; his victory over Dr Goldwitz had given him new confidence.

'Just this once. Then I promise I won't bother you anymore.'

134

Bruce grabbed his arm and twisted it playfully until John winced.

'Otherwise I'll be bothering you all the time.'

Bruce stood in front of the seated boy on the train as if to guard against his escape, but John remained motionless, his arms folded tightly across his chest, his eyes lowered as if in contemplation.

'You're not mad?' Bruce swayed above him, his shirt slipping out of his pants as he clung to the strap.

John mumbled 'No.' He would not give the bully satisfaction. Yet Bruce seemed oblivious to John's mood, and invincible. A debased god.

'The veterans are having a rally down in front of City Hall. We're gonna screw it up for them, the fascists.'

John shut his eyes. It relaxed him to think of an imaginary gun; nobody bled when he shot them: they simply fell like bowling pins.

'I've brought someone new,' Bruce said and pulled John forward roughly so that the boy stumbled and put his hands out like a blind man.

Harry grasped John's hand but feeling no returning pressure, dropped it. 'Thank you for coming. We need you. We need all our friends to show them how weak they are.' He waved his arm towards City Hall where a crowd of men were singing, 'God Bless America'.

It took some time for the Partisans to organize themselves and begin marching three abreast across the park. John lagged behind, forgotten by Bruce in his excitement at being asked to hold up one side of their banner.

The men in front of City Hall, some in old war uniforms with medals from Korea and World War II, held American flags and hand-written signs. They huddled together to sing the national anthem, too shy to face the people who stopped to stare at them. John could almost pity them with their faces as wasted as his own. He stood apart from both groups, a bystander now who could enjoy himself.

When the Partisans drew close, the veterans seemed deaf to

their chants, confused at first by the banner Bruce had helped to unfurl: 'End the Imperialist War'.

Then, more grief-stricken than angry, they shouted, 'Cowards. Commie cowards.'

One of the veterans ran forward and tried to tear down the banner, but Bruce pushed him away.

'Keep cool,' Harry said.

The Partisans drew close to each other. The girl with the frizzy hair grasped Bruce's arm and began singing, 'We shall overcome,' and soon they were all singing. Bruce had never felt such unity in them as if the girl's pure high voice came from their throats. But the song seemed to enrage the veterans who surged forward using their flags to drive a wedge through the Partisans.

They fell with their arms around each other like bruised lovers. 'We're non-violent. We don't fight.' Harry grabbed Bruce's shoulder but the boy shook him off. He pulled a man off one of the Partisans and began wrestling with him. 'Run!' Harry shouted at Bruce before disappearing through the trees.

It took four men to hold Bruce down while the others kicked and punched. He looked up to see John staring at him from beyond the inner circle of men, his white face like a mask above the grimaces. Bruce opened his mouth to call to him, but choked on his blood.

John heard sirens and walked quickly away from the circle, his hands in his pockets. He turned several times to see if anyone was following him but did not stop walking until he reached the subway entrance. And then, remembering the big boy lying on the ground, trying to avert his face from the spittle, he began to laugh.

The man of the painting's title appears only in the first picture wearing a long black coat and calmly reading the newspaper. It seems he is less important than the chairs, the table, stove and the window with its neatly drawn curtains. Yet he is all you think about as your eyes follow the three other pictures like sections of a stained glass window with their heavy black borders. You wonder why he left no evidence of his passage through that room, and why Magritte willfully painted the same setting four times as if to say that this is one moment, one moment, one moment, one.

from Madeleine Kurtz's art journals

He came from nowhere. They were standing in the middle of the damp lawn, her father holding his hat in his hand, pleading: 'Why don't we go in, everyone else is.'

But her mother turned away. 'There's Teddy.' She couldn't stop herself from pointing. She dropped her hand when he looked over at them. 'Come.' She pulled at Madeleine.

Her father grabbed her other hand. He put on his hat even though her mother told him how ridiculous he looked with the little blue and gold feather sticking out of the band. But Madeleine had stroked its beauty. Hadn't he bought the hat for the feather?

It was May but Teddy's wife wore a white fur the morning light turned blue, the color of a genie disappearing. Teddy's face was smooth as if he had been freshly molded from wax. When he gave Madeleine his hand, she felt how soft and full it was. In her stiff nylon dress, she was a cut-out doll beside their luxury.

'He's your kissing cousin,' her mother said.

But nobody did any kissing.

'Who is he?' Madeleine whispered as they all walked into the synagogue.

Her mother shook her head because the rabbi had begun and her real cousin stood up there in his white shawl waiting to become a man.

Her father whispered, 'What he is, is rich.' The word brushed against her in the gloom of the synagogue like an enchantment.

Madeleine was leaving them at the end of the summer. 'You'll be a college girl,' her father said. He had stopped traveling to stand behind the counter at Macy's selling men's shirts. Every night he was at dinner, face bashful like a lamb smiling.

She got a summer job filing at a Jewish charity near Times Square. Each morning Doris, the office manager, handed her a grey file and a box of new donor cards. There seemed no end to the benevolence of Jews.

At three o'clock, Doris brought out a tray of cheesecake and lemon tea. Irving, the charity's director, emerged from his office to say, 'Come. A treat.' Doris handed around the cake but never ate any. She was lean and black and towered over the narrow old man. Madeleine watched her long fingers pick up a glass mug of tea. How could he bear to be around such elegance? But Irving just sat there sipping his tea and smiling.

The place had a cramped feel though Madeleine had a big desk in the reception area, and Doris sitting in her glass enclosed office did not bother her once she had seen that the girl understood the alphabet and would work. Maybe it was the high small windows and sloping floor which made her feel always on the edge of a rough sea, though the only movement was the steady turn of the fan.

At lunchtime she rushed out into Times Square, letting the sunlight like a great tide sweep over her. She wandered down side streets, stopping by stage doors for a glimpse of famous actors arriving early for the evening performance. Once she thought she recognized an actor buying a newspaper on the corner where Times Square opens like a shout. He did not notice her looking at him or if he did he knew how to ignore.

At dinner her father began telling Madeleine how they were going to meet downtown for lunch, just the two of them. But her

138

mother spoke into his words: 'Guess who Joe saw downtown?'
Her father looked confused as if her voice had whirled him
round and he was too dizzy to speak.

'Guess,' she said but didn't wait for answer. 'He saw Teddy.'
Madeleine knew Teddy had moved back to the city, but she
always thought of him out in the wilds of Long Island.

'Joe said he had a girl on each arm.'

Madeleine didn't believe her uncle's story, but she imagined
Teddy sauntering along Park Avenue like an emperor, his long
rich coat carelessly open, the women clinging to him.

Her father sat side saddle in his chair, the way her mother
did because she was always getting up to bring something in
from the kitchen. She was a small woman, hair in a frizz around
her urgent face. Madeleine was taller than her but always
stooped down to be at her level.

'What about his wife?' he asked.

'She wasn't up to him was she?'

Her father turned to Madeleine. 'Like I said. You just tell
me your lunch hour and I'll make it mine. They'll give me any
time I want.'

Her mother said, 'Aren't you something?'

Madeleine told him she couldn't say when her lunch break
would be. But she took lunch the same time every day. If she
never met him, he couldn't tell her what he kept in his terrified
eyes. And maybe he would bring back all that had disappeared:
the black umbrella gone from the back of the door, the sample
bag he took around with him when he was a traveling salesman
and not a man behind the counter at Macy's. He would open it
and take out his life.

That night she kept turning her pillow, then went to the
window to breathe what little air was moving. Outside her room
someone walked back and forth. She put her mouth to the open
window, shut her eyes and thought of Teddy high up above the
heated city.

'It's gotta break,' her mother said day after day when even
the clouds seemed to burn.

One morning when she rose from the subway, the sky

139

shimmered around her, and in the charity office she could not think to put the cards in their rightful order. She found herself reading the words of donors, so many remembering the dead. But others commemorated their daughter's marriage or a son's law degree as if by giving away some of their bounty they might placate those who envied them. She wondered if Teddy would come up in the cards. But why would he give to them, to their cramped giving?

After lunch Doris put one of her cool hands on Madeleine's shoulder and told her to go home. 'It's hit a hundred.'

The heat would be worse up in their sixth floor apartment, her mother still in her house dress, the air humid with unhappiness. She remembered the little pond in the park and began walking uptown. It would be another country in there with the trees bowing towards the bridge.

Madeleine had forgotten how the leaves wore the dust of the city and the still air above the water smelled of something overripe. She had sat down on one of the benches when she noticed him across the pond. He was sleeping with his hands on his knees, his face smooth and vacant like some half-worked mask. She stared and stared and would have walked over there to make sure, but suddenly he opened his eyes, looked around himself as if he had lost something. Maybe it was the heat which made her face burn suddenly. She looked down and put her hands on her cheeks.

Teddy, if it was Teddy, had every right to sit on a bench sleeping in front of all the other sitters. Of course he would not recognize her. The last time she had seen him was at her cousin's Bar Mitzvah; she had been an eight-year-old, but he was still the same man.

He shifted around, crossing his legs. Soon he would be going back uptown to one of those buildings along Central Park with uniformed porters. Up and up. She saw him at his window staring down at the night-softened green, the city like a bracelet around the darkening trees. Later when her father sat alone watching TV and she was washing her hair, he would come out in his white suit.

He yawned and stood up. His jacket was an ugly shade of yellow, but somewhere inside it was Teddy. He began walking out of the Park. She waited, then followed him past the fountain, along 59th Street to Lexington, but when he started down the subway stairs she stopped. Teddy never traveled below. For him taxis swerved and stopped, and on the little bridge horse-drawn carriages waited.

She was quiet over dinner. Her father sat on the edge of his chair, his eyes downward. A fan turned in the kitchen sending hot draughts over the table.

'Let's open the door,' her father said.

Her mother said nothing to this.

'I said, why not open the door? When it's so hot?'

'You kidding? You want everyone to look at us?'

No not this. Her father might speak again, might ask why she was so ashamed. Because it was the only way of stopping them, Madeleine asked, 'Has anyone heard news of Teddy?' As if by conjuring up the man in a cool white suit who just now was stepping out, she could make her mother swallow her bitterness.

Her mother repeated her Uncle Joe's story, only this time the women clinging to Teddy wore jewels.

'He never settled,' she said. But Madeleine could see that his strutting through Manhattan with glittering women pleased her.

'Maybe he has too much money,' her father said.

'You should know.'

Her father managed a shrug. 'You can have too much money. After all, his father was poor. They had nothing when he was a kid.'

'Don't say "poor",' said her mother.

'He was. He came over like a ragamuffin. Didn't know whether he was coming or going.'

Teddy's father was her mother's elderly cousin. He'd been a displaced person who had arrived in New York after the war. Madeleine used to think that meant someone had taken the space he left behind. How could anyone fit his stooped shape cut in the grey air of Poland?

'But has anyone seen him? Besides that time I mean?' she asked.

Her mother said, 'Teddy lives in a different world. Nobody hears from him anymore. Even his father.'

She saw her family as Teddy might, the three of them sitting close to each other at the round table in the little alcove. Her mind went funny as if they were living in some old movie not an apartment in the Bronx. The man on the bench came, though she tried to cast him out. He just sat there with his hands on his knees sleeping.

Later she sat on the sofa staring at the TV, willing the man on the bench to fade into the screen till the black of her mind filled with the real Teddy. She wanted to say to her father who now sat with her watching that it wasn't about his money.

In the night she heard the TV on low. When she went into the living room she saw her father asleep on the sofa, the sheets up to his chin.

She was following her mother around the house. Her father had just left for one of his selling trips and her mother made the beds, one after the other. Madeleine tried to help her tuck in the sheets but her hands were too small. 'You can smooth the bed,' her mother said, 'your father always leaves a crease.'

In the office she was working her way through the alphabet. By mid-August she had reached Teddy's letter. His real name was Theodore Ruben, but she called him Teddy Ruby. That morning, after Doris gave her the R file with a stack of new donor cards, she looked up Teddy. He wasn't there, not in the new or the old. She imagined him giving carelessly the way someone might slip a coin into a tramp's hand not looking to see how much or if the tramp noticed. Not for Teddy the slavish words of these philanthropists with their remarkable sons and good dead wives.

She asked Doris, 'Does anyone give anonymously?'

Doris laughed. 'Nobody just gives. You want something in return when you give what you worked so hard for.'

'But if you're very rich you don't care.'

'Even then.'

142

'Especially then.' Irving had come out of his office. 'Especially the rich men. They want everyone should love them.' He patted Madeleine's head and went out for lunch.

'You got your answer,' Doris said.

Maybe because she gave up on Teddy, maybe that's why she saw him again. She thought he looked different from the man in the park, more haggard but still with an expression as if he were not in this world. 'Like he's waiting on heaven,' her father used to say when their waiter seemed not to see them. He sat hunched over the counter in Chock Full o' Nuts drinking from a mug. She sipped her Coke watching him. If he looked up and happened to look in her direction she would smile. She would know then.

He stared down at his cup then put some coins on the counter and got up to leave. Madeleine stood up but tried to act like it was nothing to do with him. She looked at her watch several times and shook her head as if someone would care very much if she were late. She decided to follow him till he reached wherever he lived and then she would ask the porter, 'Was that Teddy Ruben?' as if she had just missed him.

He was not easy to follow this man, stopping as he did to look in windows with his hands in his pockets, then standing idly at the corner of Times Square smoking. She lingered with him, disguising her interest by staring into the traffic as if she were waiting for someone to pull her from the maelstrom. For the first time she felt impatient with him. 'Don't you have anything better to do?' But she stopped even that thought because Teddy didn't have to be anywhere. He could loiter all day here while she sat beneath high windows plucking the names of the fortunate.

It was then staring into the crowds crossing the street that she saw her father moving with the others. He had taken off his jacket and his long bare arms hung at his sides. She drew back into the doorway. What was he doing here? He'd come all the way uptown from Macy's. He told her once that his legs still itched to travel even after he'd settled down to a store job, itched so much he had to walk through his lunch hour. He looked not

143

like an explorer, but a lost man with his moon face and white shirt. Even at a distance, shrinking from him, she could see his bewilderment.

The man from Chock Full o' Nuts had begun walking away. By the time she noticed, he was turning into a side street she knew from her waits outside theater doors. She ran to catch up, but when she reached the corner she had to follow at a distance for he seemed suddenly alert and purposeful. And then he disappeared in the shadowed street where actors arrive mouthing their lines, and idle men drink in narrow passages lit with red bulbs.

What if she cried, 'Teddy, Teddy, come out. Come out.' Teddy Ruby, son of a refugee. His father was an ugly man from a Polish village with a name like a cough who told dirty jokes and kissed her on the lips. His father was there at every wedding and Bar Mitzvah. But Teddy did not return to her.

When Madeleine came home from work that evening, winds swept through the apartment slamming doors. She walked through the house calling her mother. The windows in her parents' bedroom were wide open. She called again though there was no one. She stared out the window as if she might see them, her parents flying together. Down below the winds swirled a woman's dress, picked up her words.

What if her father was hiding like he used to when he came home from one of his trips and she had to make him appear? She rushed through the house again calling 'Mommy, Daddy' like some foolish child who thinks their parents gone if they're out of sight. She began opening doors to closets one after the other, till she reached her father's, the dark cave he hid in beneath his coats and suits, the shelf of his hats. But it was light now and she could see for the first time the rough walls, the long pole with its jungle of wire hangers. She could see it all because there was nothing. Nothing he'd left of himself.

In the evening Madeleine sat watching her mother eat, her head bent low over her food. If she didn't ask her mother might never say and then in film winding backwards her dad would appear in his best hat with the golden feather. She looked at

Madeleine. 'The heat's broken. Finally.'

On her last day at work they held a little party. To the cheesecake and lemon tea they added little glasses of schnapps and marble cake. Doris said to her, 'How you did it. The cards, every day the cards. You are a patient girl.'

After waiting so long for the end of summer, Madeleine began to feel the pleasure of nostalgia. She thought of the first days when Doris frightened her. She could look years ahead and see them gone from the room which tipped around her as she drank from the little glasses.

Irving kissed her on the forehead and brought out a package wrapped in silver paper. Madeleine had never expected a gift. She tried to open it neatly, but the paper tore.

Doris said, 'That's it girl.'

The bag of bright blue leather with stiff little handles was a present for a child.

'Open.' Irving nodded his head.

She struggled with the clasp. Inside in the satin folds she found a silver dollar, like a promise from one of the benefactors.

Madeleine left the office and descended into the brilliance of the afternoon sun. The schnapps gave her a strange 'I don't care' feeling. She kept thinking the words, 'and then she did not go home', as if she were both herself and a stranger. She walked into Times Square, stood on the corner where Teddy had lingered with her and then began to stroll uptown till she reached the park. She would have gone home then but for the sight of a woman just like her hesitating at the entrance. The woman shrugged, then crossed the street and left the park behind. How easy it was to turn away from longing.

When Madeleine entered the park, she felt her heart quickening. She told herself she didn't have to go, but her walk was no longer languid. She might miss him and then never see him again because she was going away.

There at the pond was the man on a bench in a white jacket reading a newspaper. She walked towards him but as he looked up she saw in his tired eyes the resignation that had never been Teddy's.

The man moved to give her room. She did not want to be near him but could not be cruel. His jacket was worn, and there was a bad smell around him.

Madeleine sat waiting till she could leave again. She drew out the leather bag and began opening and closing the clasp till her fingers hurt. It made a little noise each time and finally he looked up from his newspaper. She thought he would beg for money but he looked into her face with his woebegone eyes and asked, 'You lost something?'

'You hear what Teddy said? He remembered me. Me. From when he was little. He looked so well,' her mother said.

Madeleine heard her father mumble, 'How should he remember?'

'He took my arm as we were going into the shul.' Her father said nothing to this. 'You hear me?' her mother said.

'You were to him like anyone.'

'What do you know?'

'I know a liar.'

Madeleine stared down at the sidewalk so she could be sure to step always in the center of each square. One step in and one step out, her legs stretching across. When she took the hand near her, she did not realize that it was not her father's until she heard her mother laugh. She looked up to see the soft smile of a man in a lopsided jacket. As Madeleine pulled her hand away, he turned towards a door with a red neon sign and disappeared down its passageway.

I remember the day they first came, for I had seen the fox. Right on Pelham Parkway, a man stood under the elevated train holding him on a ragged piece of rope. A husky fellow and poor. You could tell by the clothes, not just that they were worn but old-fashioned. The fox lurched forward, yellow-eyed, thin, his heart-face full of terror. Even if the rope broke, he could not find his way back along the sidewalk past the candy stores and the delicatessens to the woods from which he was stolen. I wanted to say to the man 'put him back in the wilderness' but I could see from his broad beaten-in face that the fox was his pride.

Someone was taking a picture of the two of them. The man did not pose but he seemed pleased. The fox retreated from the camera and stared at the group gathered on the sidewalk with a trace of his old slyness. But he had been mastered by the man who soon lost interest in the photographer and our questions and began walking away, the fox stalking behind him, for even in captivity a fox does not lose his manner of walking.

It was a Saturday. I had bundles in my arms: frozen vegetables, meat, my shirts from the dry-cleaners. I had to do it all now since my wife pushed me out. Her shrink told her I made her crazy, all those years she hadn't realized till he said it that it was not her insides which were rotten but me; she'd only married to escape the rancour of her family. I had stopped traveling by then and settled down to selling in Macy's menswear department. For her I did it but she said men of my generation were not such failures.

I did not care what she said to me, she had always talked so, but to my daughter she whispered till the girl was ashamed when she saw me behind the counter. My daughter went to college, the first in the family, and then moved downtown to an efficiency apartment near the Battery, a filthy little room with a hotplate she preferred to our comfortable apartment in the Bronx. She won't see either of us now. I gain some satisfaction from knowing that Gertie hurts and cries like I have done for years. I want to say to her, 'You think you could turn her against me, could ridicule my life without dirtying yourself?' Yes it is the only satisfaction. When I dream now it is not of Gertie coming back to me smiling, with the sarcasm gone from her lips or even of a new woman in my bed, but of a daughter, a faceless girl whose hands caress my face, press my eyelids till I sleep, who listens to my dreams like fairy tales.

After the divorce, I moved to this stumpy brown building which faces another, my apartment on the fourth floor always in shadows. I knew when they came in the elevator I should get out but my arms were aching from the bundles. I wanted only to put my key in the door, my food in the icebox, pour my drink and sit in the living room with the curtains drawn thinking of nothing.

They were lounging in the elevator, the stupid one leaning against one corner, the other holding the chrome banister with his hands behind his back, his chest thrust forward like a girl's. He glanced at me but looked away when I stared back. I saw a message travel between them, some movement of their heads and then I began to get nervous. But it was too late. We were at my floor, they had seen me press the button. If I did not get out they would know I was afraid, so I pushed open the elevator door and they followed behind me.

I stopped in the middle of the floor. I thought I'd get back in, pretend I forgot something, I would look stupid, but hadn't I always played the fool? But when I paused the dark thin one pushed me forward. 'Go in.' When the other drew a knife, I lost my head, I began to scream, only the sounds which emerged from my throat were hoarse whispers of 'help'. The blond broad-shouldered fellow held the knife before my face till I grew silent. The dark one told me to hand him the keys, and he opened the door and pushed me in. I was still holding my bags, but the shirts had slipped from my hands onto the floor. He stepped on them as he walked by me. I remember thinking at the time that I was glad the dry-cleaner had carefully wrapped them in plastic sheets so he could not soil them.

'C'mon,' the blond one said, 'give it to us.'

I handed them my wallet but that did not seem enough. The dark man wandered into the bedroom; I could hear the drawers of my dresser being pulled out. He returned empty-handed and looked at me with a queer smile. He looked educated, the dark one, and he spoke differently from the other, in a cloying tone as if he could wheedle my treasures from me. He was neat, a trim dark beard, close-cropped black hair, leather jacket and dungarees tight around his serpent body. Only his eyes blazed with the disorder and violence which the other wore about his person.

'There's more,' he said to me. I was mesmerised for a moment by his look as if he had witnessed my most intimate dreams.

'C'mon,' the other shouted.

I remembered I had twenty dollars in my cuff-link drawer but that was all for I did not like to keep lots of money about the house.

But they wanted something else, something which I did not know I possessed. The dark one searched the apartment while the other stood watching me. He returned with my watch and the pearl cuff links Gertie gave me when we were first married. He stalked around the living room, picked up a photo from the top of the television.

'Your daughter?'

I don't know why I said yes, it was stupid of me, and then he looked at the back and saw 'Madeleine, Graduation 1968', for my wife always liked to name and date the pictures. She was very orderly that way.

You wonder why I didn't call the police after they left, was I such a coward? They had threatened me but it was not that which stopped me, but what the dark one said about my daughter, how they would find her. They knew my name you see from the cards in my wallet. You think it farfetched? They said they would search for her, no matter what, even if they spent years in jail, they would nurse their revenge. 'I never forget,' the dark one said. So I kept quiet and they knew for they returned without fear in their faces.

During those weeks after they left I did not like to talk to people for I worried that I might blurt it out, so I kept away from my neighbors. I used to listen by the door for the sound of their voices in the hall, for the opening and shutting of apartment doors, for the choking of the elevator as it approached our floor. I did not go out much, only to work, to shop. I moved quickly in and out of my door as if the outside world might rush in and swallow me.

It was the beginning of November when they returned, the early darkness like a vast pool waiting for me at the end of each day at the store. Crossing the street from Macy's with the streetlights full in my face, the night already around me, I felt invisible, no, not invisible, but without substance, as if only the borders of my self existed like a figure in a child's coloring book, just the black outlines of my coat and hat, my cuffed pants, my shoes, the night filling the empty spaces of my groin, my belly, my heart, my eyes.

I had a system by then. When I approached the building I made sure no one was around before I entered. I moved quickly through the little hall, peered into the window of the elevator before opening the door, then with my heart pounding I pushed the button and willed the elevator to start moving before anyone could rush into the building after me, and then willed it to move past the floors without stopping.

That day all went smoothly and I emerged on my floor, the hall empty and quiet, the brass doorknobs like burnished faces surrounding me. I made for my door, clutching my keys. I had taken them out when I entered the elevator so as not to waste a moment. Then I heard the creak of a door, the rush of feet and they were upon me. They had waited in the back stairs, the fire stairs we called them. I had only ever used them when the elevator broke down. They pushed me in the apartment, hit me over the head and I fainted.

They were still there when I emerged from my stupor. They had dragged me into the living room. I saw them on the couch dividing one large bag of white powder into smaller ones. I shut my eyes again and pretended to be unconscious. They were talking as they worked but it seemed another language to me, 'cutting this with that', 'stashing the stuff', 'smack and junk', words like knives.

The dark one said, 'We'll use this place to hide out.'

'What about him?'

'We'll see.' And then almost as if he sensed me listening, the dark one tapped me with the point of his boot. 'Wake up.' Still I pretended to be unconscious. The blond one shook me till I hurt so much I could no longer pretend.

They had put the bags of white powder away somewhere. The dark one was staring at me while the other tied me up. Then they went into the bedroom and I could hear them talking for hours. I must have dozed off for when I woke the blond one was untying me and the other was whispering almost endearingly to me, 'Now you keep quiet about all this 'cause we'll be back.' He flapped the photo of my daughter at me, 'I'm taking this, so you see I've got her.' I watched him put the photo inside his jacket. 'Close to my heart.' He winked at me.

The other said 'C'mon Jeff, stop fooling around.'

They shut out all the lights in the apartment before they left. When I looked at the clock in the kitchen it was five in the morning. I went into the bedroom but could not sleep in my bed for their bodies had been between the sheets. The blankets were twisted, a small empty bottle of whiskey lay on its side and cigarette butts were scattered about the parquet floor. They had been through my dresser again, the drawers lay open like so many mouths, my pyjamas and underwear dangling from the sides. I thought I'd be sick for the room smelled of animals penned up for too long.

I sat upright on the sofa, my arms by my sides just as they had been when they bound me. My legs grew stiff and cold in the morning air, the speckled darkness swept over me when I shut my eyes. As the corner of sky left by the hard lines of the building opposite grew light, I thought, they have taken my daughter, my scornful child, they had her picture to mock, to soil, to show again and again to robbers like themselves. My mouth formed the word 'No' and the numbness left me. I stood up walking on dead legs, shaking dead arms, moaning when the pinpricks began.

I called in sick that day and stayed out the rest of the week. When I returned to work, Charles, the new man under me, a young fellow straight out of high school, dumb but eager, told me I looked washed out. 'Maybe you need a vacation,' he said. I coulda kicked him. Still, during my coffee break I went to the men's room and looked at myself in the mirror for a long time. Did I look changed? I was thinner maybe; I had nicked myself shaving and the bloody gash stood out against my pale skin. I heard the door open so I started combing my hair.

'Seen a ghost?' Ed Flowers, a husky guy my age who breathed like a heart attack was coming. I had always looked down on him. He'd spent all his life behind the counter at Macy's. I used to say to my wife he'd die there, topple over the white shirts he sold day after day. Now I was thinking he'd probably outlive me.

Somehow I knew they'd return, it was like having cancer. You forget about it for a while but you can't escape, it comes back and back. I knew they hadn't finished, that the dark one was hungry still. They invaded my dreams, men like them who came in through huge gaps between the door and ceiling, through broken windows, through doors accidentally left open, sometimes even through the keyhole, like demons. And in my dreams they came with large grey dogs, the kind with small pointed ears and rectangular heads.

Someone was after them. They'd come in the night, then disappear before morning, then return two days later. They took my key and made copies for themselves, that was at the beginning when I was still leaving the house, going to work. You wonder why I didn't change the lock but what difference would it have made? The dark one said to me, 'We've got your number.' They were with me all the time, bound to me even if they didn't want to be.

They continued to bring their drugs, for that is what they were, the brownish leaves, the white powder. They did not care anymore if I saw, for they said I would never talk. The dark one, Jeff, glided about the house, his lean arched body ready to spring. 'Speak to me,' he would say when the other left the room, 'you never speak.'

Stevie, the one with hair like straw, a broad face like a Polish yokel, liked to twist my arms with his thick peasant hands and slap me when I did not move quickly enough. Jeff would watch, his arms behind his head, his body comfortable against my sofa. I wondered why they did not kill me but then they needed me as time went by to buy them food, to answer the door. I thought they were becoming foolhardy. Could I have had such logical thoughts then? They began going in and out during the day; though they kept out of the way when the doorbell rang, they must have been seen by people in the building.

At first they wouldn't let me answer the door or phone but then Jeff thought the neighbors would get suspicious. And sometimes it was their friends at the door, come to take away the heroin or smoke the pot with them. They talked about the drugs in such detail, it was all they talked about except for girls, Stevie boasting about 'balling' this one and that one while Jeff listened with a smirk on his face. Stevie brought a girl back one day, I hardly saw her go by. They were in my bed while I was tied up in the living room. She came out with him. All I remember about her was the tall shiny white boots she wore and her eyes looking at me like I was some odd bird at the zoo. Stevie was saying something to her I couldn't hear. She laughed but continued to stare till he hustled her out.

I don't know when it was I stopped going to work, when I stopped shaving, when they kept me most days in the dark bathroom. I could feel my beard growing in the moist darkness as I lay curled up in the bathtub.

Testimonies

We all knew. We saw these bums walking in and out of the place like they owned it. Sam wouldn't know that kind, never Sam, such a quiet man, gentle, too soft for a man, my neighbor Hele used to say. 'He lets them in, doesn't he?' she said. 'So w'

153

are we to interfere?' As if Sam wanted such filth in his house. But you know these yentas, they have to know everything that's going on, but they don't care about anyone.

The others were afraid of the two guys, afraid that if they called the police, their names would be revealed in court. I have to tell you I was afraid too. Somebody even suggested that Sam was a homo and these guys were queers. 'His wife threw him out didn't she?' Better not to get involved, what my mother used to tell me.

Then we didn't see him for a while and when I did I got a shock. His hair had gone white and you could almost see through his skin; with his thin long beard he looked like something out of the Bible. Maybe they had sent him out to get food. He didn't speak to me, not even to say 'hello'; he did not look me in the eyes when I said, 'Sam what's happened to you?'

***

I figure he was after his daughter. After he peed on himself we threw him into the bathtub. He made me sick just to look at him. I said to Jeff, why don't we just stick him, what's he got to live for anyway? And then we got no one to tell stories on us. But Jeff wanted to play with him, he always had to have someone to play with.

***

He didn't mind us being there so long as we didn't touch his daughter. He had nobody, I could see that, but when I asked him about himself, he wouldn't speak. He acted like we were the same. Stevie's just an animal, a pure animal, couldn't he see that? I wanted him to tell me how it felt to have us there, to see me handle the photo of his daughter. I wanted to hear what was going on in his head when we tied him up and then untied him. He was just a dead man when we met him, we knocked some life into him.

154

I went away for a while to a hospital, then a nursing home still in a wheelchair. They said it was the shock made my legs buckle when I tried to stand up. They taught me to walk again. The nurse said it's all a matter of confidence. But I was still shaky when I returned home, so Macy's retired me early. I can't complain, they were generous and the boys even got together and sent me a check for fifty dollars and a retirement card with a picture of a fat man playing golf.

I wouldn't have told my wife, but she heard from one of the neighbors. She felt pity and came round to see me when I got home. Madeleine too. They flocked to me, to my carcass, for I was no longer there. They may speak to me, stare into my eyeballs, even take my shoulder as I walk them to the door, but I have fled my body. It happened when I was lying in the bathtub, my hands tied behind my back, a heavy rope round my bent legs, my face in a puddle of bath water. My mouth opened and my soul bubbled out. I sank in a greenish pond below the water lilies my daughter used to pull when we took her to the botanical gardens. I used to tell her to stop, the sign said not to touch, but she was always saying it was a tug of war between her and the lily and she couldn't let go till one of them won.

I was always an anxious person, all my life dreading what I could not name. Each time something bad happened, I'd say 'It's finally come, it's finally broken over me', but never so. My next-door neighbor Ethel Kaplan was sick as a dog from speaking in court. She said she didn't recognize me after they got through with me. Now she avoids me, I know she listens at her door for the sound of mine opening before she ventures out.

The judge said they tortured me, turned me into an old man. How could I tell him, they set me free?

She had come before. A tall full woman with milky arms who ran her fingers over the backs of his chairs. Saul watched her through the curtains shielding him in his office at the back of the store. There on the long rough wooden table he'd covered in brown packing paper he was eating his roast beef sandwich and reading the newspaper.

He gave her a few minutes to leave because customers came and went quickly when they came at all during the summer. Who wants to think about upholstery and carpets in the heat? And Saul did not want to be seen lolling around so he stayed in the little office, hot like the sultan's cave.

But she was standing in the middle of the diamond-shaped room looking towards the back as if she could see him sitting there with his half-eaten sandwich and new green pickle. He wiped his lips and moustache and came through the curtains.

'You have some nice things,' she said, lifting the swatches from a high-backed chair with curved legs and arms. 'Can I?' she pointed to the seat.

'Of course. Try it out.'

'So uncomfortable. But that,' she indicated the stocky tweed sofa with fat cushions, 'that is not so pretty.'

It was part of his American set, the hodgepodge most people chose. Though the store was only one room, Saul arranged the furniture as if there were several. To these he secretly gave names: French Provincial, Italian, Danish Modern. Each consisted of an armchair or sofa, and a coffee table with ornaments or a lamp.

She had an accent, not strong, but he could tell she was from the other side by her clothes: the long polka dot fitted dress with the raised shoulders, the hat like a half shell. Who wore a hat on a hot afternoon on Gun Hill Road in the Bronx?

'You want maybe some new chairs?' he asked.

'I want everything. But what I need I don't know.' Then she

pointed to the glass canister filled with hard candies in colored wrappers. 'Can I?'

Downtown the showrooms had bowls of silver wrapped candies which he rolled around in his mouth as he strolled through the airy rooms. His sat there for years, and no one had ever asked to have one.

'If you want,' he said.

'But are they real?' She laughed. 'I'm so dry,' she said putting the candy in her mouth with her eyes on him. Then she was walking around again. 'So much in a little place.'

He said nothing to this. When his father came over from Poland, he became an upholsterer who filled the store with brocade and satin. Sometimes people got confused and asked Saul to make a slip cover for their old sofa. He spoke sharply to them, 'It won't be me making it you know.' He was not an old man sewing in the back room.

He had to stop himself from saying to her, 'So what is it you want?'

The women, how they played him. 'I like that and that.' They'd point to a modern loveseat and a rich brown French provincial table. When he explained that these could not share the same room, much less sit within a few feet of each other, they said, 'Well I like them together. And that's that.'

He'd paced what little floor space existed between the furniture. 'Then why ask me?'

'You're too fussy.'

'What do you mean? I see hundreds of homes.' He did not. It was rare a customer asked him to come over and give advice.

The woman walked over to the Italian set, the brass lamps with their large silk tasselled shades growing out of round marble tables. 'Too ongepotchket for me. I like simple but not so simple.'

If she were not good looking, he would have said 'Let me know when you've made up your mind.' And he'd have gone to the back room to wait for her to leave, because some of the women wanted only to talk.

'Could you come over?' She looked at him. 'Tell me what

to do with my rooms.'

'I would have to charge.'

'But of course.'

She took down his number and promised to phone him.

Saul wandered around the store after she left, smoothing down the swatches she'd picked up. He thought she was not serious.

Then he went back to his office to finish his sandwich. In the heat of the dry windowless room, he longed to go out and play handball. He could almost hear the sound of the small hard black ball against the concrete stone wall in the playground. When he was young his hands were calloused from playing. He moved, his friends said, like a monkey around the court, but as he grew older he began to lose games. It was not his body which slowed down. It had remained firm, lean, his own flesh did not hold him back, but what had attached itself to him: his daughter, his baby son. Their faces appeared on the edges of his vision, distracting him as the ball flew towards him.

When she called nearly a week later, he had almost forgotten her. He was drinking a ginger ale and turning the pages of the newspaper, so quiet back there that the sound of the phone was like an alarm in his sleep.

Her accent seemed stronger on the phone. Even her name, Lottie Saltzman, sounded like some grandmother or an aunt who had come over later than everyone else. 'I told my husband I was having the interior designer come over. "Oh big shot," he says. So you'll have tea with me and then we'll talk.'

Normally he went to customers' houses in the evening after he closed the store. But then he would have to tell his wife to hold back his dinner, and she would want to know everything.

Lottie lived in one of the heavy old buildings on the Grand Concourse made to look like mansions with carvings of angels and curlicues on the doorways. Once the rich lived here and now those who made more money than he did. As he walked down the long dim corridor with its tiled floor and brown doors, he thought of what his wife would say: 'Old, so old it makes me depressed.'

159

It was cool in Lottie's apartment as if the walls of the building shut out the day and all its heat. He could see a hallway where the bedrooms lay, room after room in darkness. She took him down to a sunken living room where the floors were parquet and the big sofas wore chocolate and crimson covers like fat emperors. The only brightness came from the table lamps and a little yellow chandelier.

He looked around as she left to make tea. In the deep of the room he felt like he had entered some wondrous cave and who knows that she wouldn't come back wrapped in sheets of gorgeous silk.

The tray shook as she walked in her high heels. He watched the dress move on her body, how when she bent over to put down the tray, he could see the smooth whiteness of her breasts and the fine drops of perspiration on her neck. The tea was in glasses with silver filigree holders, and she pushed a gold-edged bowl of sugar cubes towards him. He had only ever seen sugar cubes in fancy restaurants.

'So have you thought what you want?' He always asked first but in the end they listened to him.

She placed one and then another of the cubes of sugar in her tea and sipped it delicately. 'I'm not born here. So I don't know how people make their houses.'

He asked if she had lived in the apartment long.

'What is long?'

He shrugged. He had lived in his corner of the Bronx all his life. Even the apartment his wife loved because it was new and modern was only blocks away from the playground where he had first seen her.

'I want not to move again. If I make this place good, maybe then we stay. Before I came to this country, well, I am moving all the time.'

He feared she was losing her words and soon would speak in some other language. He didn't like to ask about the other side, where she had come from before, who she had been in that place. He had a second cousin who'd been in a displaced persons camp after the war and laughed all the time.

'I would bring big colors in here and modern furniture. You see I want to banish all this brown, color of mud.'

'Modern would not fit in this older apartment.'

'Saul. May I call you Saul? You must know one thing. That I cannot be sad.'

'Who's saying you'll be sad? You'll be sad with loud colors.'

'I'll be sad if I have any more brown.'

'Who said you have to have brown?'

'Then we agree.'

He sipped his tea. It was too hot for him but he could not do what he did at home which was to blow on the tea till its surface scudded with his breath.

She said she would have to phone to arrange the next time. 'Because Aaron. My husband. He'll tell me we have somewhere to go, so I cannot know ahead.'

He asked what Aaron's line of business was, though he did not want to know. She had met him when she came over after the war, and he had made sure that she could stay. He was a lawyer.

Saul imagined Aaron much older than her, a balding lawyer she married out of desperation.

'Aaron's like you. A real American.'

He handed her some catalogues. 'Once you decide what you want I can go to the showrooms just to have a look.'

'Showrooms sounds very grand.' She smiled at him.

He shrugged at this, feeling for the first time irritation with her. It was true that he rarely went down there where dapper young men wandered about with their customers. The showroom assistant would come up to him to ask if he needed help, but he always shook his head. He was just looking, getting ideas for someone fussy.

Lottie did not phone for two weeks. He figured she had changed her mind. Maybe she was just toying with him, or lonely for company till her husband returned in the evening. Saul had occupied one of her dead hours.

One afternoon when there was heavy rain which came and

161

went so quickly that the air outside never cooled, she walked in laughing, her hair dripping. She had been up in the Catskills at a hotel. 'All day it's eat, eat, eat. The old men play cards in their bare chests, and at night some little man comes on and tells dirty jokes. I was so tired from being bored.'

'But you got away,' he said, his hand touching his moustache, rubbing across it with one definitive gesture, as if to say finish with this talk of expensive hotels. When he took his family up to the Catskills, they stayed in a bungalow colony. His wife cooked and sat on the porch of a wooden cabin holding his son, while his daughter went off to day camp.

'Who wants to? Don't you feel when you're away, how could you have left? But maybe you don't go.'

He was thinking of the lake water on the first day, how when he dived in it cleansed him. 'We go up there in August. You take a deep breath of the mountain air and let out the Bronx.'

'I like this air,' she said smiling at him.

He came over later that week to do some measuring and talk about furniture. He sat on the brown sofa in the sunken room while she served him tea and little square cakes she gave a French name. The icings of pink and white were so sweet they made his teeth ache.

'One thing I cannot get used to. The cakes here. You see them in the stores with names like cartoons. I am fond of cake. And you? Maybe your wife bakes.'

He laughed at this. 'She's no baker.' What he wanted was his usual Danish, chewy and just sweet enough, which his wife bought every day from the Italian bakery. The smell of it when he pulled it out of the wax bag.

He gave her some rug swatches to choose from and got out his tape measure and pad. He was down on his knees in the corner measuring. She came over with the rug samples cradled in her arms. 'I am lost without you so I'll wait.'

He looked up at her. She seemed so voluptuous in her black and white checked dress, her legs in shiny stockings, her bare arms moist in the dim light.

'You narrow down what you like.'

162

'What I like you won't.'

'You're the one living with it.'

Lottie sat down on the sofa in the place where he had been. Saul kept going around the room, measuring and writing. Then he could no longer delay going back. He looked at the high, hard chair, but went instead to sit beside her.

'Maybe this one because it makes me think of cornfields.' She handed him a sample of a green carpet flecked with gold.

'What do you know of cornfields?'

She blushed and looked at him. Suddenly he was putting his arm around her and she was not moving away. He could pull her towards him, all her flesh, her milky arms, her breasts inside the black and white dress, her long neck moving like a snake when she swallowed. He looked at her face, and in the dimness of the room she looked unfathomable.

'Are you making a pass? That's what they call it isn't it? Isn't it Saul?'

'I'm sorry,' he said.

'I'm flattered. If that's what it was.'

He wanted to be gone.

She leaned back against the sofa. 'We are getting to know each other very well. I would say to you that there is something I cannot do here. I cannot be alone with myself.'

He felt chilled as if he were underground in the sunken room, a step below the rest of the flat and the hazy end of the day. He began sketching the room on a piece of graph paper and writing down the measurements.

'Saul, you want we should talk about it?'

He shook his head, still writing. 'You make your decision, and then, I'll order.'

'I've embarrassed you,' she said.

He continued to write and sketch. 'Here. I've added the size of your sofa. You want the same size? And the armchair too?'

'I want all new,' she said. He thought her eyes looked teary, but could not be sure because the room had lost its bit of afternoon light.

He nodded. 'Next time you will tell me for certain. You

must be certain because once I order, that's that.'

She placed the money for his visit in his hand, then closed up his fingers. Her hand, long and lean, was not what he expected from the rest of her. Then she let go and smiled again her teasing smile, just like the first time in the store, as if he were the greenhorn not her with her wobble of an accent.

He told her that after next week he would be away with the family. 'The store closes,' he said, as if it had a mind of its own.

'So you will come back a new man. How will I know you?'

'I'll be the same man,' he said. He was thinking of the first day back, unlocking the heat of the store and the dust gathered in his absence.

She walked him to the door. 'Don't forget about me up in those boring places. I will count the weeks and be at your store just when you come. Just then. You cannot escape me.'

It was something for him to know that he could return to this cool place with her. They shook hands and then she leaned over and gave him a kiss on the cheek, soft like when his daughter kissed him goodnight.

And then he could not help himself. He took her in his arms and held her so close that he could feel her breasts and belly. When he opened his eyes, he saw that she had never closed hers. She looked wild and lost, and he let her go.

Saul did not return refreshed as he had every summer. He'd felt restless up there sitting on the porch eating barbequed hot dogs, the woods like some dark curtain behind him. His daughter came back from the day camp crying because the girls formed a club and wouldn't let her join. His wife said one day, 'Why does it always have to be mountains?'

In the store he had less time to sit in the back room and remember Lottie because customers were starting to order curtains and slip covers for their worn-out sofas, now that they could feel the breath of winter. Sometimes he didn't even think of her and then he did.

He worried that she had forgotten him again. He had disappeared from her mind, like her memories: 'I am every day burying and then like a dog digging them up in my dreams'. A week passed and then another. He wondered if she remembered when he was getting back. Then he thought she had been playing with him after all.

One day when he was eating his sandwich in the back room, he heard the door open, and when he looked through the curtain Lottie was standing there.

'Saul?'

He came out still with his shirtsleeves rolled up.

'I'm sorry,' she said.

'You changed your mind?'

'I was ill.'

'Well I'm sorry.' He didn't believe her. She looked as full as ever.

'I was very bad you see.'

He nodded but he didn't see.

'I had to go to hospital. Yes. Well that's over with, but what I come to say is we're moving all the way out to Long Island. My husband thinks it will be better for me in a real house with what you call a lawn. He says the Bronx is going down. But I don't think so. I think I will be a hausfrau out there.'

'That's where everyone wants to live,' he said.

'And you Saul, you want that too?'

He thought of the boys around him hitting the ball against the wall, hitting and running and the taste of the sooty air, the Bronx taste. 'If I could manage it, yes.'

'Oh well. Maybe you will move out there and become dull like everyone.'

'You'll never be dull,' he said.

'But dull is what we all want. No?'

She puzzled him still. What made her sadder than everyone? It made her different this shadow she clutched to herself.

'My husband said why keep thinking about over there. When you're here.'

'He's right. What's past is past.'

'You think that? You don't.'

'I wish you luck in the new house,' he said.

She took his hand. 'You know what it's like? You say goodbye and you know that you will never see that person again.'

He shook his head. 'That's not the way it is here. You'll come back for a visit, at least.'

'I like you Saul but what do you know?' She shut her eyes, and he put his arms around her even though they were standing there surrounded by windows in the diamond-shaped room. He held her like he did his daughter when she had a fever and was afraid.

He let her go, and she was smiling again. 'I'll be seeing you. That's what they say, isn't it?'

Saul went back to his sandwich, his newspaper folded neatly beside him. He read and ate and when he finished he thought he would rearrange his room sets so that it was obvious what was what. Too many of his customers went from French provincial to Danish Modern without blinking their eyes. He would show them you could not be both. And when they tried to mix the two, he would show them what peasants they were. Peasants.

But who was she or what was she? He rubbed his eyes.

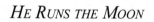

He Runs the Moon

She called and called: 'Mr Silverman. Mr Silverman, you can come in now.' No one stirred in the dim waiting room. Perhaps he was dozing, sunk deep in one of the soft high-backed chairs, but the only presence was an arc of dust shining in the last sunlight. Miss Wick stood for a time quite still, then she shook her head and turned sharply back to her room to check the appointments book.

Yes, Mr Silverman was down for five o'clock. It was twenty past now for she had been so long scraping the plaque from Mrs Richards' molars. Could he have come and gone? But she had not heard the bell deep in the brownstone, mournful like the last tones of midnight.

Patients waited sometimes for months to become one of hers and when the appointment card for an annual cleaning finally arrived they rarely asked to be changed to another day. For Miss Wick, the dental hygienist, was as revered in Cambridge as the college which stood like a castle beyond the swirl of traffic. She and Dr Williams, the ancient dentist, one arm swollen with arthritis but the bright eyes of a boy scout, had worked together for thirty years. 'I see Dr Williams's handiwork,' she would say looking into a patient's mouth: 'His fillings are like pieces of art.'

She could remember when Harvard boys wore suits and ties, when the panhandlers moved in and when one day during her lunch hour she had been tear-gassed. Just like that she heard what sounded like a low bomb, then running, a great wall of young people and she too running, her eyes tearing so she had to make poor Miss Edgerton wait a half hour for her clean.

Purgatory they called her room. Her patients peered up at her as she scraped and picked, polished and flossed. 'You're lucky,' she said to Mr Delmore after she had worked over his mouth for nearly two hours. He had not been to the dentist since he was child. 'You were given strong teeth. Now you take care of them.'

He looked up at her, tears of pain still in his eyes, his mouth bloody: 'Can I go to heaven now, Miss Wick?'

She loved the children best, loved teaching them the brush strokes, warning them about the tooth dragon. But it was Miss Wick they feared, her eyes like Fourth of July sparklers, her bright bright smile like a triumphant fairy. The only color in her gleaming white presence was the translucent red drops she wore in her ears. So bright, so luscious, someone joked they were made of blood from her patients' mouths.

'I just don't understand it. He seemed such a nice young man. Not even to call and apologize.' Miss Wick paused to let Mr Mackey rinse his mouth. The blood ran freely into the cup, a sign she was getting down to the raw teeth.

'Maybe he was embarrassed.' Mr Mackey was a big man with the face of an archangel. 'I would be.'

'Ah, but you wouldn't do such a thing, would you?' Miss Wick sprayed a jet of water into his mouth before he could reply. 'This young man, and I won't name names. That wouldn't be fair. He just never appeared.'

Mr Mackey was the fourth patient she told about Mr Silverman. Mrs Booth, who was a hairdresser, called him a 'no show'. 'We get them all the time. Some people are completely thoughtless.'

Miss Wick shook her head. Not her patients. Only emergencies kept them away. Mrs Barry who had labor pains two weeks early and didn't have a chance to cancel, even she had written a note of apology from the hospital. And once, when Mr Wood forgot, he sent her a dozen red roses.

Miss Wick waited two weeks before asking the receptionist to send Mr Silverman the bill. When it came back promptly with his check, she gained no satisfaction from knowing that he had to pay for a 'no show'. He had not written a note, not even a scribbled apology.

She brooded on his face, but the more she tried to conjure him up, the less she could remember: sandy-haired, glasses, a suited young man. She had moments while she was running dental floss through Mrs Jacobs's shaky front teeth or scraping tartar from the wisdoms Mr Oakland insisted on keeping, when his face became clear again, so clear she stopped what she was doing and shut her eyes. Then he was gone, and Mr Oakland looked up at her. 'What is it? Have you found something?' Because Miss Wick could find holes Dr Williams missed.

She thought he might relent. She invented excuses for him: a death in the family, an accident. But the face which surfaced was free of such cares. A pleasant enough face.

'Why don't you call him?' Miss Sobel said, 'if it's bothering you.'

Miss Wick cocked her head to one side and smiled. 'Oh, but I couldn't do that.'

Miss Sobel blushed and started to apologize, but Miss Wick's hands suddenly darted inside her mouth. For Miss Wick did not phone patients. The few times she had been too ill to come to work, the receptionist called everyone to cancel.

If she heard his voice perhaps then his face would stay with her, perhaps the voice would tell her why he stood her up, why he could not even bring himself to apologize. For his face was fading from her mind. Sometimes she could not even be sure if he was fair or dark-haired, whether he wore glasses, whether he was twenty-five or thirty-five.

She woke in the grey hour before dawn to see a ghost head. She shut her eyes and tried to conjure him, but the ruddy faces of her brothers appeared, quiet as her patients while she talked to them. They had been her babies, two fat dolls placidly staring up at her. 'Geraldine is a natural mother,' her mother said.

'Oh well. Why don't you just strike him off,' Dr Williams said.

'Don't you think I should speak to him first?'

'If you want to go to all that trouble.'

'But just imagine it. Not even to call.'

Dr Williams rested his arthritic arm on the back of the black vinyl chair where his patients lay back and opened their mouths. He regarded her with a smile. 'Have you never been disappointed, Geraldine?'

171

If she heard his voice, what could she say? It had been nearly a month, too late to ask if he was okay, if he was alive. One of her patients had died the day before he was to see her, but his wife had written.

She could send a note: 'Mr Silverman if you do not call to explain your non-attendance, I will have to take you off my list of patients.' But he might not call. What if he were so hurt by her scolding words that he turned even further away from her? She could word it differently: 'Mr Silverman, after your recent non-attendance at an annual cleaning, I wish to know whether you still want to be kept on our list.'

She did not send it to the receptionist to type but wrote it out herself with her fountain pen. She slept through all the grey hours of doubt, woke at dawn, sharp and brilliant as the metal instruments with which she probed her patients' mouths. She addressed the envelope, was slipping in the note, when she thought, suppose he asks to be kept on the list and then does not show again? No, it was not possible. Think of the money, his teeth. Yet she knew she would wait all year for him to come. Even now in the full sunlight of her kitchen, she'd begun to dread him.

'Forget him Geraldine,' her mother's voice. 'He's not important.'

Her stomach turned and she could not eat her breakfast: the two triangles of toast, poached eggs cooked to firmness, the coffee, black and bitter.

'If you do not eat, you will feel faint.' Her mother's scolding.

I am not your little girl anymore. I'm not anyone's girl.

She was dull that day, making conversation about the weather, silent during the whole of Mr Appleton's hour. The beaver with his small sharp teeth, his hairy face and shiny eager eyes. After she scraped off his year's accumulation of plaque and tartar, after she had polished till the yellow faded, after he had rinsed and spit, rinsed and spit, he said, 'I feel like a new man.'

But you have not changed Mr Appleton. You will come to me in a year's time, your teeth covered with your bad habits.

She said, 'Now you must take care of your teeth as if they were
your treasures. Floss twice a day, remember.' She did not pat
him on the shoulder the way she usually did her men.

'Yes Miss Wick. I'll be better.'

But Miss Wick had turned away and was staring out the
open window.

She tasted the ocean up through car fumes, the sweetish
tang of salt and death her fishermen brothers could never wash
away, and she must drink and drink again. Not for years, not
since she had stopped her monthlies had she known such a
thirst. But it was the Charles River she tasted, the 'dead sea',
its brackish waters so filthy you could not dip a toe in without
needing a tetanus shot. Years ago she used to walk down there
during her lunch hour, a slow promenade to help her digest.
Then the vagrants came and she had to skirt round the lovers
tumbling behind dusty bushes, the men curled like babies on
the wooden benches crying in their sleep. The grass grew weary
and yellow, and she could find no more life down by the river.

On the street she could not smell the Charles; the air was
rich with chocolate chip cookies, croissants, coffee. She strolled
with the rest of the lunchtime crowd past cafés where young
men and women drank foamy coffee, picked at delicacies and
gazed at her. She had left her sandwich in the office for this was
going to be just a quick walk to clear her head; now she wanted
what these coffee drinkers ate. In the crowded cafés she would
have to share a table, so she walked on till she reached a narrow
street of crooked iron stairs leading up and down to little shops
and cafés.

All higgledy-piggledy. She shook her head and smiled as if
to one of her recalcitrant patients. She was almost at the river
when she saw *Seville*, a basement café where a lone couple sat
with their backs to the street drinking wine. A burly man with a
guitar looked up at her when she entered but continued to pluck
the strings.

She chose a side table and waited. The man with the guitar
eyed her again but looked away when she smiled her Miss Wick
smile and nodded encouragement. Perhaps he could not bear

to look at her, his eyes so accustomed to shadows. For she was like a beacon, a shrill light on the greenish pockmarked walls, the broken black and white tiled floor, the lone poster of a dark-browed woman twisted in dance. When he finally came with his pad, she thought, what a sad man.

'I'll have a ham sandwich and coffee.'

'What kind of coffee? Espresso, latte.' He stretched open his hands to show the enormity of her choice.

'Just ordinary. I'll have whatever is ordinary.'

Miss Wick ate, then leaned her head against the rough wall, lulled by the strumming of his guitar.

Just by pushing the door in her bedroom she was on the other side. Bare, dusty, with a ceiling stretching up like a cathedral, how could this room be part of her small bright apartment, her soft bed like a nest under the low ceiling? She searched for the door but it was above her now in the vaulted shadows. She dug her nails into the wall and tried to climb. 'I'm trespassing,' she tried to shout but her throat closed on the words. The door was too high and as she reached for the loose wooden knob, she slid down.

How long she had slept there, she could not say, but she did not wake feeling bright and ready as the morning. It was as if a slimy sac covered her body, but within her heart was pounding. She looked at her watch. She had slept past her lunch hour, well into Miss Stern's one o'clock cleaning.

She wiped her mouth with a tissue and searched the shadows for the man. The couple whose faces she had never seen had left. She pushed the table forward, then clung to it for a moment till her head cleared. She began to walk back towards the kitchen.

'Sir,' she called out, 'I would like to pay the bill.' She pushed aside the bead curtain but there was no one in the long narrow kitchen. Then she heard him coming from some room beyond, some labyrinth deeper than the cavern where she stood.

When he emerged at the back of the kitchen, she noticed that his shirt was wrinkled, his face bleary.

'I didn't want to wake you,' he said.

all the difference, someone hung up. It happened again and she began to understand.

Then I will change my habits for you Mr Silverman, I will surprise you. She skipped days, called at different times, sometimes when she arrived home, or just before she slept and once when she woke in the middle of the night. The woman answered, her voice thick with sleep and fear. 'Not you I want,' Miss Wick wanted to say, 'no need for you to be upset.'

She began to chat to her patients again. They heard the stories about the glittering fish her brothers caught, the purity of the Maine waters, but there was an urgency in her words, a breathless quality which made them fear her long white hands moving around in their mouths.

And then it happened. Always she had to catch him off guard, so one night she ate dinner early and called before doing the dishes. The phone rang and rang. There was a pause before a voice came on. She couldn't even tell if it was a woman or man. The voice told her that no one would come to the phone and to leave a message. She sat there holding the receiver, listening to silence until she heard a click and finally a dial tone. She called again and again, counting the rings till the voice came on. She moved her lips but spoke to him only in her thoughts: I know you're there, Mr Silverman. She waited an hour just sitting by the phone before she called. When she heard the voice, she had to cover her mouth to keep from screaming his name.

She went straight to bed after that, leaving the dishes, for she could not keep her eyes open. Her sleep was dreamless, long and heavy. She woke after the alarm sounded, yet she was still tired. All day she was silent before her patients; she wanted only to sleep.

It was lucky she had the weekend. She slept through Saturday and Sunday, pulled herself to the phone to call in sick on Monday. Just some virus she needed to shake. She could not eat, could hardly stand, her bones worn and pitted by an ocean swelling in her ears. She shut eyes and floated out above the murmuring city.

The telephone woke her. 'Hello. Hello?' Dr Williams

177

sounded embarrassed. 'Geraldine?'

She thought she had answered, but the words were only in her mind. 'Yes,' she whispered.

'Are you all right?'

'The day. What day?'

'Friday. When we hadn't heard from you all week I thought maybe something was very wrong. Are you okay?'

'Then I haven't left after all.'

'Geraldine, do you think maybe you should see a doctor? Sometimes flu can develop into something serious.'

'I am weak. That's all.'

'Well. It sounded much worse.'

'Just something I have to shake.'

'When do you think?' He stopped. 'You come back when you're better, you hear?'

She wiped her eyes. He need not be so kind to her.

'My patients,' she whispered.

'Don't you worry about them. We'll just cancel all your appointments.'

She wanted to say 'No, no, tell them I'll be there', but even sitting up to talk to him was too much. She dropped back on her bed and shut her eyes.

Now it was grand, the other room, with patterned walls of scarlet and purple, heavy velvet curtains held back with golden braided ropes she'd only ever seen at the museum, and kingly sofas covered in damask. She understood that this was her room. She might live in it instead of the modest square spaces she slept in and ate her meals. Mine, she thought fearfully, mine.

Her name was Grace Tomasino, but we called her 'the tomato'. Plump and rosy and smiling, she liked to lie on the bed, eyes shiny while she sang along with Ray Charles: 'I can't stop loving you'.

Everyone in the dorm knew about her summer in Europe, how she had met Vince, an Italian waiter on the boat going over, how he had followed her all over the continent. Now she waited for the letters which came from New York, Marseilles and Naples.

'Tomato! You got something,' one of us would call up the stairwell and she would become alert, then rush down the stairs as best she could in her fluffy slippers with the high heels. He sent her little gifts: a leather purse marked with the word 'ciao', a small cut-glass heart on a silver chain, and at Christmas a card with a picture of a blonde Madonna.

Grace became an orphan at six when one after the other, her parents died of cancer. They were wealthy and left their estate to their only child on condition that her aunt and uncle be guardians until she was twenty-five. She never thought of them as blood relations; they were keepers of the gate to a world she longed to enter. They found the little girl spoiled and unruly, and when she moved in to their house they imposed rules for her to break, punishments which we had only heard about in novels. After they saw her holding hands with a boy, they locked her in her room for days. She did not tell her guardians about Vince; they would say he was just after her money and forbid her even to write to him. We never saw the aunt and uncle though they lived close to Boston, but we believed in their cruelty, for how else could Grace have been so enchanted?

At first Grace went with us to Harvard mixers and laughed at the boys who took her phone number; her Italian waiter was a man of twenty-seven. She began to stay home on weekend nights and waited up for us to come back from blind dates

179

screaming with boredom. In her long silky nightie with a collar of translucent wings, her full cheeks pink from the overheated room, she was our plump fairy godmother. We went to her for cups of coffee, for embraces when we could find none elsewhere. She had only one story to tell, so she listened closely to us, chuckling or sighing as was appropriate, offering us sticky Italian nougat when we were depressed.

In the Victorian brownstone dorm we were all friends, but Grace talked most to Laura Stone, for she had also spent the summer before freshman year in Europe and found the college boys gawky creatures compared to the Frenchmen who kissed her everywhere but on the mouth, the Israelis who declared there was no sex in America before leading her down to the darkening beach. Laura sat cross-legged on the bed, her narrow back arched, her pouty mouth forever moving, while Grace lay stretched out beside her. They'd stop speaking when I entered the room, Grace looking at me with an indulgent smile as if I were a child intruding into the parents' bedroom.

Once she stayed with Vince when his boat came into Boston. They spent the night in a dive of a hotel while we lied to the dorm mother. After she came back, I heard her talking to Laura: 'But it's a safe time, isn't it? Isn't it?' Laura saying: 'I was late once. I thought I'd die.'

In the spring while we marched two by two up to the State House demanding the right to abortion, Grace began to plan her escape with Vince. She told only a small circle of friends within the dorm. When I look back, I wonder why none of us asked her why she could not wait at least till the end of the semester. We were seduced by her affair, so little like the paltry embraces we knew. More, I was reminded of the romances in the fat novels by Tolstoy. Laura looked disturbed, I thought, because she was being upstaged by her friend.

My roommate Gwen and her boyfriend drove Grace down to New York to meet Vince and they got married on the boat. 'I couldn't believe he was the one at first,' Gwen reported. 'He's got teeth missing and he's at least thirty-five. But so charming. He treated her like a princess.'

We were all silent for a moment. Then I said, 'Well at least something's gone right.' Heads nodded and we all went out for ice-cream sundaes. We were celebrating the triumph of romance, the completion of Grace's year of work.

Grace's aunt came to the dorm to question us. A neat woman with a dry, practical manner, she reminded me of my high school gym teacher. As she sat on Grace's bed she looked each of us in the eyes before saying: 'She's ruining her life, don't you see?'

Still we refused to tell her Grace's whereabouts, but someone must have spoken in secret, for the aunt and uncle followed her to Italy and were able to get the marriage annulled. After they brought her back, a broken queen, she swallowed all the aspirins in the house.

Before I left Boston for a summer of silent battles with my parents back in Connecticut, I visited Grace at a mental hospital, a private one beyond the city on high wooded ground. She had graduated to the open ward and sat before a square white table as if waiting for an interview, her head lowered, hands clasped, her tongue moving inside her cheek as if searching for some lost treasure. Her hair was held back by pink combs, and she was dressed like a schoolgirl in a white button-down blouse and plaid skirt.

'They told me not to go around in my nightie,' she said.

She came to visit us during sophomore year, still dazed from the electric shock treatments. I took her arm and we walked past the auditoriums where she had slept through lectures, the classrooms where she'd sat mooning about Vince, but she could remember nothing, not even the names of the professors I greeted in the hallways.

'Should I know him? Don't tell me.'

Laura passed without seeing us, but Grace suddenly broke out of her somnolence and ran up to the tall sallow girl and hugged her.

'I didn't recognize you,' Laura said after she disengaged herself from her tearful friend. And then she began to talk about

181

her Israeli boyfriend. I left them there on the sidewalk, Grace entranced, smiling up at Laura.

Grace promised to return to college but she never felt strong enough to begin again, and after sophomore year we forgot about her. There were other elopements. Gwen went to live with a graduate student she'd shared a couch with one night after a war resisters' meeting. Sue dropped out to marry the boy she'd clung to from high school.

After graduation I crossed the river to Cambridge to live with a group of friends on a street they called 'neighborhoody', where children played in bare front yards and the fumes of a candy factory sickened the air. I got a straight job in a bank. I came home to the smell of marijuana and burnt pork chops, and lay on a sofa covered with someone's cast-off Mexican shawl listening to the Mothers of Invention.

I did not recognize Grace when I met her again. She called out to me from behind the scarf counter at Filene's. She'd lost weight, had shadowed her soft blue eyes in violet and wore a wig of long black hair.

'I knew you immediately. You look the same,' she said, laughing at my innocence.

I was for the first time afraid of her; I did not want to be drawn in again. She told me about the musician she was living with in an apartment in Back Bay. Her guardians did not speak to her except to tell her that the jazz man was after her money.

'But how can he know? They're crazy. Anyway, he doesn't need the money. He's dealing.'

We exchanged phone numbers, but she never phoned me. I entertained my housemates for an hour with her story, and then she was forgotten once again.

I began to go to consciousness-raising meetings where women would give testimony against their boyfriends, their husbands, their fathers, where declarations of abstinence were made and then broken. 'I know I have my pottery, my plants, my politics, but I need something else,' a woman pleaded.

I came away from these meetings vowing never to marry. Not that men were distasteful, but I did not want to be burdened with disappointment, to have to chant a litany of complaints before the solemn women, so like the mothers of my childhood, who confided to each other while their children played, and then returned home to put a pot roast in the oven.

Laura appeared at one of these meetings, sitting cross-legged in the inner circle, offering confessions when she could. She did not see me, and since I did not offer up bits of my life to the group, there was no need to make myself known to her. When she spoke she never commented on the woman who preceded her, offering sympathy or advice, but launched into her own story. She was in love with a man, a famous musician who was living with her best friend. What should she do, what could she do? He had come on to her. She was so alone and he was, she paused as if struggling for words, he was so talented. She made us feel the erotic sympathy between them, how natural they were together, how the best friend was a dull woman who giggled when Laura spoke of feminism.

'I love her, of course, but she's so backward.'

'Talk to her,' a woman said when she could get a word in edgewise, but Laura shook her head. 'Impossible. She wouldn't understand.'

'But she's your sister.'

Laura glared at the speaker. 'It's not my fault.' She turned to the rest of us. 'Is it? I mean, she doesn't even have orgasms.'

Much later I learned that the best friend was Grace. She knew nothing until she came home early one day from work to find Laura wearing her nightie, trailing around the house behind her boyfriend who was stripped to the waist and blaring on a saxophone.

'I picked up a kitchen knife. Really. I tried to kill her.' Grace giggled. 'Well that's done with now. You remember Vince? He's married some village girl half his age. The dirty old man.' But she looked sad. 'They have a child. I know because he sent me a picture last Christmas. He still sends me cards every year. He calls me his first wife. Isn't that nice?'

She was 'the tomato' again in a pink fuzzy sweater which only she could wear, her fine blonde hair falling out of a bun,

183

her face glowing with the pleasure of seeing me. We walked through Harvard Square, our arms around each other, heedless of stares.

Grace has her wealth now, and she's settled down with a businessman in a large ranch house up in Revere. I imagine her slow dancing by herself in the living room, her feet slipping into thick white carpet like fresh snow. Then she's preparing coffee for the women on her street, who come the same time every day to her warm house with the rose walls and the ashtrays shaped just like the Bay of Naples.

I remember the Sunday morning she first appeared, the hot pools of sunlight on her desk and on the stone urchins in the garden where she wandered.

I sat alone in the members' room looking at her through the open doorway. She was like some translucent insect with her wispy blonde hair and pale thin arms, but her face was Botticelli, not beautiful, just full of light. When she saw me watching, she walked inside and sat down. She seemed to listen with me to the opening of doors all over the museum and the first footsteps of the day.

Before she came I never talked to the others in the members' room. We sat on padded wooden armchairs reading or writing or in the case of the old sisters staring. The only chatter came from the two large wooden desks at the far end of the room. One was for the secretary who presided over the room on weekdays. Miss Randle was an upright Irish lady who liked to joke with me about the ne'er-do-wells in her South Boston family. The other desk belonged to the Ladies Committee, a group of suburban women dedicated to the betterment of the museum. On Sundays some pale boy student sat in Miss Randle's chair taking memberships and reading. It seemed only the ladies could sit at the desk of the Ladies Committee.

I don't recall anyone ever checking to see if we were bona fide members. It was just assumed that no one else would dare to come in. And the room itself showed us how to behave; newcomers soon learned its laws of silence. And awe. Because just outside the doorway was a massive Pharaoh, stern and still in his first death.

This new girl sitting at Miss Randle's desk stared as each person came in. What did she expect of us? Maybe she thought we talked to each other. I was for nodding at regulars, but the old sisters were forever nodding, and in the end I wanted the silence. I had been a starry-eyed architect before being bumped up to manage a whole city department because no one could forget I'd gone to Harvard. Now, as my wife says, I'm doing what I want to do, spending my retirement days inspecting the handiwork of the Egyptians.

We heard her take the first student membership of the day. The pale boys had simply looked at the college ID and written out a card, but she asked questions: Are you, her voice trembled, are you an artist? I thought that in time she would learn silence. The student left the room with his card; these youngsters never sat with us. She was back to staring around while her fingers made twists in her hair.

When did it start, her little club of those who sat before her and poured their hearts out? I stayed back from this, but wanted to warn her about the guards. On the first morning they came to see her, the big guy with a face like a peeled potato who stood in the room nearby, and the head guard, a small man with a look of intelligent amusement. She thought that once they left she was alone with us, but there were watchers from the beginning.

After she'd been there a few weeks, one of the members of the Ladies Committee appeared. I knew Jane Abbott back when she was beautiful, drunk and heedless, and I pushed a guy into the Charles River who was trying to make her. We spent the rest of the night in my car. She gave a nod to my hello. I guess nobody likes to remember they've been wild. She's become one of these gaunt white-haired women who sit on committees and play golf, all her laughter contained in little sardonic looks. But her drinking continues.

'Are you all right dear?' she asked. But there was no affection in her voice, in the hard face with hair so firmly swept up that it looked like a stone headdress.

The girl just sat there with her hands in her lap while Jane began opening the drawers of first one and then the other desk. I have known these women, these descendants of the righteous of Salem, since I was a child. My mother was one of them. Rummaging through this poor girl's desk was just to show her that she possessed nothing in this room.

She sat very quietly after Jane left, then got up and walked into the garden where she stayed for a long time. I was about to go to lunch, but I watched the room in her absence, watched for the face of the guard, but only the woman who cleans the toilet wandered in.

When she returned, it was with a serious face. She took the next membership without saying a word beyond what was required and lowered her eyes when I smiled at her. I wondered what she did the rest of the week. She could not live on these Sundays.

The next week she was back looking at all of us and it was only a question of who would pick up the bait of her eyes. The first to breach our silence was the 'study in brown', a stout woman of middle age with muddy colored hair who came most Sundays and ate her lunch in the room. This was probably against the rules, but she ate with so little fuss, gathering the crumbs around her mouth that no one noticed.

She went to the desk to renew her membership, but stayed talking. I could not hear much of what the girl said, but the woman's voice came to me. Why did she let it out so quickly, her widowhood and awkward daughter? The room was so quiet that her words came as if through the hush of a theater. The girl seemed not to mind. She turned her face up to the woman, played again with a wisp from her badly managed hair. When the woman finally got up and turned, the girl smiled as if someone had given her a precious secret.

Did she have a favorite? It could not be the grizzled man who sat angrily turning the pages of the museum's magazine, he of the work shirt and paint-splattered jeans. Of course he was an artist. He told her how once he had painted on a nude woman, just painted all over her body.

'And then?' she asked, so quiet her voice.

'I made love to her,' he said, his head shaking like some aged lion.

Nobody looked at anyone else. I felt like kicking him.

She laughed and looked wise.

One bright Sunday morning a man in a black suit with the domed forehead of a judge, about my age but bulkier than I would ever allow myself to become, came in to get a

187

membership and started talking. He took off his heavy black glasses as he spoke as if without them he could see her better. I heard enough scraps to know that he was telling her the story of his never lived life. 'But what do we know?' I heard him say. I did not hear what she replied. When he got up to leave he said, 'goodbye Miss no name'. We never saw him again.

But the regulars continued to have their session with her. The 'study in brown', whose name I learned was Annie, now ate her lunch sitting opposite the girl. The artist continued to court her, but he had quieted down, and sometimes he would just sit there silently picking at his fingernails.

The girl. How many Sundays had passed and I still did not know her name though I tried to give her one: Chloe, Diana, Phoebe, but none were right. The two sisters and I were the only regulars she did not know.

'I just can't make up my mind whether to move. I know I should. What better place could I find?' Annie was up there eating her sandwich. The artist had arrived and was waiting his turn. I heard the girl say, 'Listen to the house. You must always listen to the house.'

Maybe I was mulling these words over because I didn't notice Jane Abbott approaching; tall, narrow and dry as a desert snake, she must have slithered into the room. Probably she was the head lady of the committee if there was such a one. I say that because she sat down and began writing with all the seriousness I've seen in minor bureaucrats. Annie looked uncomfortable but the girl continued to talk now with her hand over one side of her face as if to shield herself. Jane made a phone call in her bright voice, then stared at Annie till the poor woman got up and gave her excuses.

Jane swivelled her chair towards the girl. 'Linda, isn't it?'

'Lena,' the girl said and then repeated her name as if Jane might take it away from her.

'Bless you,' I mumbled to myself. Now I don't have to name you anymore.

'There's been so many of you I just don't remember. Where do you go to college?'

'I don't,' she said.

'So,' she paused, 'so Lena, what do you do?'

'I come here.'

Jane Abbott smiled that awful smile of cocktails and side whispers. 'Yes, you do, and I hope you are not too bored.'

Poor Lena. Did she not realize what Jane was saying? That she was not to talk to members. Then she looked through the drawers of Lena's desk, even pulled out a bunch of envelopes.

Lena watched Jane gather herself. She waited till it was clear that she was not returning. Then Lena did something I could not believe.

No one else in the room saw her pull open the drawers of the ladies committee desk, one by one, open and shut till she found a bag of Japanese rice crackers one of the ladies had left behind or perhaps kept to snack on. Lena tore open the bag and began to eat the crackers. Noisily. She saw me watching and before I could drop my eyes, she came towards me with the bag.

I shook my head. She went round the room offering. They did not know it was not hers to offer. Soon they were all eating crackers, except for the ancient sisters who looked bewildered. She returned to me. 'Come on,' she said. And I knew I must join this communion. The rice cracker was shiny and brittle and as I crunched it in my mouth I thought of the ladies, even my mother, of their bones.

There was a change in her after that. She seemed determined to break one rule after another. We came one Sunday morning to find her sitting on the edge of her desk smoking. No one had ever smoked in that room or sat on the desk or stood combing their hair.

When students came to buy their membership cards, she waved away their IDs. I thought how sad it was that we would soon lose her. We would never discover what she did during the rest of the week.

But she stayed. The little head guard began to make an appearance every Sunday, sometimes with potato face looming behind him. Though these visits were made with a casual air, I knew they were prompted by Jane Abbott. Only she would think that curbing the chitchat was more important than guarding the treasures. During these five minutes, those who had always wanted to touch the Pharaoh could put their moist fingers in his eyes.

They always came in the morning, around the time when the two sisters arrived fresh from their morning coffee in the cafeteria. Lena sat upright in her chair. She could not flirt with potato face, but the other one she could charm or so she thought. He reminded me of the men who ruled Boston city hall when I first worked there, whose jobs had been handed them by fathers, uncles, grandfathers. Their good humor masked their anger, for they knew what everyone knew, that they had not earned their place.

We understood not to approach her till this visit was over. The room relaxed in the afternoon when one after the other we sat with her. Even I came to lounge in the soft chair. What was it about her which made all of us not worry about being boring? Who else would listen to my obsession with the Egyptians or discuss over and over again the decisions of Annie? Who else would let the grizzled artist court her in the most graceless way? Maybe it was the museum itself which made us forget ourselves.

I still knew nothing about her. When I asked if she herself was an artist, she asked me back the same question and in the confusion of my answer, I realized she had not said. She did not sound Boston. There was something singsong in the way she talked as if she had drifted in from bluish hills.

'Why do you love them so much, those Egyptians?'

I don't know why I answered her the way I did. Usually I would talk about their history and the beauty of the tombs, but I said, 'Because they wear their faces like masks.'

One morning she came late, her face desolate beneath the strange striped knitted helmet she wore. I thought she looked hung over but maybe it was something else made her stay with her head on her folded arms like a child at school told to take a nap. The phone rang several times before she could be bothered to pick it up. I knew it was one of her personal calls and not someone phoning to ask about joining the museum because

190

she was listening and nodding. Did she never tire of being a confidant? I heard her say, 'They drive me crazy, all of them.'

I imagined her in some chaotic house of young people like the one my youngest daughter lived in for a time in her last year at college. Poor Lena had to succour these people as well as us and probably clean up their leftovers. Then it occurred to me that she meant us.

I kept my distance though early morning was my time to chat with her before most of the others appeared. I was reading some monograph so I didn't notice that the old sisters had risen till they had reached the middle of the room. They moved slowly and in silence. They only ever got up to go to morning coffee, lunch or to the ladies. At the end of the day they would still be there facing each other while they put on their little fur coats, as if one had become the mirror for the other.

There was only a ladies in the members' room, an odd inequality born I guess from the needs of the Ladies Committee. But the sisters continued to walk past the bathroom door towards Lena who stared at nothing. I wanted to shake her from her pale misery. Didn't she realize what a big moment this was for the sisters? They had never spoken to anyone in that room. Then she woke. That's the only way I can describe the change in her as if warm blood coursed through her once again. She gave them one of her smiles. I knew then that we did not drive her crazy. We were her court.

Lena pulled up another chair but both of them stood in front of her desk, like ancient schoolgirls in their pleated skirts and pageboy hair. It was a simple question one of them had about the next exhibition. From what I could hear, for I had become an eavesdropper, they were worried that they would not get into a lecture on Russian icons.

'Because we have Russians in our family,' one of them said. 'Russian blood,' I heard the other say and was pleased at how odd they'd turned out to be. I knew their family a bit. They were about as Russian as I was. I could see just by looking at the sharp features beneath the flesh of their age that they, like me, had descended from the Puritans who dug the rocky soil of

Massachusetts and knew no pleasure.

They grew silent when she asked just where in Russia their grandparents came from. Then one of them said, 'We never knew, never.' I don't think Lena believed them but what did it matter? They had finally spoken to someone else of the jewel which sat between them when they ate lunch and shone above as they lay dreaming in their separate beds.

It was the Sunday after the Russian exhibition had begun. The somber old halls wore the clothes of passion and bleeding, and icons loomed in dark cases. Two young temporary guards stood among the red and gold tapestries as if stupefied by them. Genuine Russians who traveled with the exhibition wandered about like living dolls to be stared at. In those days, when there was still a Soviet Union, we thought of them as forbidden. One of them had found his way into our room and then to Lena, a slender gremlin-looking fellow with slanted light eyes and fine blond hair. He could have been her brother but for the way he looked at her.

He wanted to show her the exhibition so I volunteered to watch the desk for her. 'Go. Enjoy yourself for once,' I said.

'What about you?'

'I've seen it.' It wasn't my kind of thing and I disliked the crowds. She smiled and shook her head as if to say that there was more to it than just 'seeing it'.

I became their watch during those weeks of the exhibition. He took her hand as they strolled out of the room, and once I saw them kissing in the alcove formed by the back of a stone lion. After she returned he would come to sit on her desk talking and smoking, his voice surprisingly deep. She barely had time for us, so entranced she was with him. One morning after a storm, I saw them throwing snowballs at each other in the garden. I imagined them as sprites in some cobwebbed woodland wearing only the mist.

The guards came as usual in the morning, but members of the Ladies Committee appeared more often because they were helping at a special information booth. Jane Abbott and her kind were in and out of the room, opening up drawers, calling each other on the phone.

On that last Sunday of the exhibition he came to sit with Lena in the room. They held hands across her desk, even kissed in front of all of us. He was flying back to Russia that evening. There was so little of her, I feared she might not survive his going. I remembered what it was like to lose someone; I never want to be so torn up inside again.

They both stood up, his hand still on her. She walked into the ladies room and he followed, so fast it happened that I almost believed it had been a film I'd watched and not quite understood. Did the two sisters see? They sat staring straight ahead with no change in their faces. Annie and I looked at each other. It was as if we formed a magic circle against anyone coming into the room.

They were in there a long time but we heard nothing. Annie kept looking at me, her worn face filled with tender worry for Lena. I thought of shutting the door to the members' room, but the ladies would still come in. Annie walked over to me. I think it was the first time we were face to face. 'I can't rescue her,' I whispered.

'Please,' she said, 'please.'

'Then go in there.'

'I can't can I? There's only the one toilet and they've locked the door.'

I shook my head. Then I saw Jane Abbott walking fast into the room.

She made for the desks and stared at Lena's empty one.

'She's in the bathroom,' Annie said.

'Oh well.'

She sat at her desk tapping her fingers as if counting the moments of Lena's absence. There was such quiet in the room. Annie kept looking at me. What was I to do? The little fool wanted to get herself thrown out. Any moment the two of them would emerge.

Suddenly the two sisters rose and began walking in their slow inevitable way towards Jane Abbott. With all their eccentricities, they were still her kind of people. They were going to tell, and there was nothing anyone could do.

Jane Abbott was talking to someone on the telephone in her high bright voice. The two sisters just stood there waiting for her to finish. It was so silent in the room when they finally spoke. 'We're Russian. Did you know that?' one of them asked, while the other whispered, 'Russian blood.' Again and again the one repeated 'Russian blood' while the other talked nonsense about her mother's face and the icons.

She could not shake them. They clung to her desk, clung through the unlocking of the bathroom door, his appearance and then Lena's. Jane never saw him, how could she through the two sisters who continued to stand and talk and talk in their halting way? When Lena came round to her desk, the two sisters began their slow journey back to their chairs. There was no sign that anything had happened except that Lena had no shoes on.

I never discovered the intentions of the two sisters, or whether they even saw Lena and her lover go into the ladies. How could they not be shocked, those elderly maidens?

Next Sunday I arrived later than usual. I felt woozy when I woke so I was slow about getting ready. My wife told me to get back into bed, but that isn't my style. By the time I reached the room, the others were standing together actually talking to each other. I heard Annie say to the artist, 'Maybe she's sick.' The two old sisters stared at the empty desk like lost children.

I sat down in my usual place well away from them and near to Lena's desk. Maybe she had gone with him. I liked to think of her disappearing like the pale spirit she was.

When the head guard poked his head in, Annie asked, 'Is she all right?'

'She's not coming back.'

'You mean you fired her,' the artist said, 'you couldn't wait to.'

'Why would we do that?' He gave us one of his smiles as if to say, 'What do you know about her?'

I felt stifled in there. Maybe this was the start of something for me. When I got up to go outside, Annie stopped me: 'I wanted to tell her I'd made up my mind. I will move. Just like she said. I need to shed myself to grow. You think we'll ever see her again?'

Lena said silly things but once she asked me, 'Don't you want always to be leaving?'

I walked around and around the garden beneath a feathering of snow. I know I was looking for her out there among the urchins with their white caps. What do we do now with the lives we gave her to hold? Then I turned and looked back into the room at Annie, the artist, the two sisters more unfathomable than any icon. I saw them take their places again when the guard left, saw my own place empty of me.

And then I went in.

How it happened? One Saturday morning I'm turning the pages of the newspaper, Carlton in the shower singing 'It had to be you', me sitting sideways at the kitchen table. I read 'When the President flew into China, he was greeted on the tarmac by the skeleton of a bird from the Jurassic age.' It was a little while before I realized that my eyes had strayed, and I had joined up two different articles, successfully it seemed. When it happened again I wondered if I could do this every day but the thrill was in the unexpected. It made reading a newspaper like dipping into a fortune-teller's mind and finding in that murky crystal ball some truth that could only be seen through a special dye.

Carlton and I lived at the top of a dull green clapboard house in rooms which seemed to pitch and heave. The floor buckled, the walls slanted and above my bed a casement window caught the moon between its bars. The kitchen was narrow and yellow and had at one end a black shower stall. When the vapors from our soups joined the clouds from the shower we had our own weather in the flat.

We were chance companions brought together by our Brazilian musician boyfriends. Carlton was English with a dose of Irish which accounted for the way he could pull wry faces and still be melancholy. He called me the whirling dervish, imagining from my olive skin and slanted-down eyes that I was the daughter of Persian magicians, but I had nothing exotic in my mixed-up Protestant Jewish parentage.

We met after our hearts had been broken and this was our talk. Actually I felt exhilarated after my Brazilian went back to Sao Paulo. But I didn't at first connect that light-hearted feeling with liberation from the cold Latin heart which beat like a slack drum next to me. And it was necessary for Carlton's sake to be bitter and desolate.

His Brazilian was still around, flinging his long honey-colored body at women. 'I'm his otherness,' Carlton liked to say. Paulo's curly hair and shapely arms could be seen in the windows of coffeehouses around Harvard Square. He had never had much English but his few tentative lines 'How you are? You would be coming?' were like golden balls to all the fleet-footed women of Cambridge.

I wanted to introduce Carlton to my newspaper game but his talk was of Paulo. Carlton enticed him with feijoada, a heavy black Brazilian stew which he had learned to make from pork and black beans. It had a look of old menstrual blood but for Paulo just the mention of his native dish made him drop whatever woman he was speaking to in his smiling, halting way. He would come for one night and then leave as if for ever the next morning.

I got in the habit of reading cross-eyed hoping for another chance encounter in the newspaper, but couldn't continue to fool myself. I grew restless and began to wander the streets of Cambridge on weekends while Carlton lay across his bed with the glossy photographs he had taken of Paulo.

One moonless night I met a psychologist sitting legs akimbo on the exhausted grass of Cambridge Common. We had one of these high-falutin' arguments about education and how students could be molded. He asked me would I like to go to the Brattle to see *Smiles of a Summer Night* which he'd seen and dissected. Haven't I seen it, well I must.

It seemed important to go out with someone just to finally break with my Brazilian, so I accepted. Maybe beneath his narrow, petulant face was someone else. But the someone could not keep his hands off my mind. When I scratched my head as we sat drinking the thick grounds of our Turkish coffee he said 'mental masturbation'. In the dark of the movie theater he whispered, 'You keep rubbing your hands together.'

To this I shrugged and rubbed harder.

'As if there is a penis between them.'

'You wish,' I said.

I shook off his probing little fingers, left him where I had found him in the darkness of the Common, and as I sauntered up the road to our flat did a twirl just like a dervish but without the full skirts.

Carlton was sitting on the floor of our kitchen with large photos of Paulo spread out around him. He had on his glasses and was flashing my scissors. His feijoada no longer lured, for Paulo said in his inimitable way, 'It was but now not' to Carlton's offer of dinner. Perhaps one of his women had learned how to make the fetid stew.

It became a scene of carnage with Carlton cutting right through Paulo's godlike face, the perfect lips which could speak such inanities. He cried as he cut and I cried with him just thinking of my Brazilian and how I had wasted a year sitting in clubs up in Revere listening to him play 'Satin Doll'.

When Carlton calmed down I suggested we gather up all the pieces and chuck them; then he could wash and go to sleep. There's something companionable about our kitchen set-up where he could be under the shower and talking to me as I drank my tea.

He began picking up one and then another of the cut-up photos.

'Let me,' I said. But he was sorting through them till he found the piece with Paulo's torso. Just the torso like some kind of glowing relic you see propped up in a museum. He took it back to his room to keep. Who was it plucked the heart of a poet from the flames of his body?

Then he stood under the shower, not even drawing the curtains properly, so I could see his white body like a ghost under the lines of water. I gathered the rest of Paulo quickly before Carlton could change his mind, threw the pieces with the remains of the feijoada into the bin and for good measure took the whole thing down to the garbage cans in the basement.

'Well that's that,' I said to him later when he sat at the table in his bathrobe drinking lapsang tea. But maybe now was not the time to tell him how happy he would be.

Carlton couldn't sleep until we talked through once again how Paulo had failed him, how he was not a complete man, would never be. Really we should both try to abstain for a while to cure ourselves. We had loved broken-up men, men who were always in the next moment, whose eyes, even Paulo's limpid ones, could never focus on us. My Brazilian if ever I had his full attention gave me a look of pure coldness as if I was the stranger in this land.

It was two in the morning before we could settle in our rooms, and I had to be up early to teach illiterate men. Carlton had one of his physiotherapist exams where he manipulated the jointed arms of a large dolly.

Next day I was half dozing while Samuel traced the letters of the alphabet, sighing quietly. 'Bad,' he whispered when capital B came up, and 'Real bad,' when he hit 'G'. The little ones he called 'rascals'. We stopped just before 'R' to give him a breather. The Read-to-Read Center provided juice and cookies just like grade school. Sometimes I felt we were all back there together and it was just a matter of time before we played duck, duck, goose and laid our heads on the table to nap. But the men who sat cramped in school chairs had never stood mouthing words while the teacher pointed or sounded those rascal letters with their child fingers on the pages of their reader. Nobody's white except me and Marion the missionary, a twinkly-eyed elderly woman in a red suit.

Samuel was the oldest, a genial man who worked all the years since he came up from Georgia on the stations of the MTA. 'I was diving north before all that fooling around happened,' he liked to say about King and the Freedom Riders. What he really wanted was to be able to write his name and read the destinations on the trains.

Marion was doing phonics with an enthusiasm I can't muster. The guy she's been tutoring has begun to pick up sentences and pretty soon will be reading on his own. He'll be getting his wheels, we say like mothers teaching their kids how to ride their bikes and then watching with tears as they whiz away from us. Only Samuel, slow and cloudy eyed, will never leave me.

I tried the first reader. Normally I'm a whole word teacher. Today nagged by Marion's good works I had Samuel sounding each letter until a word emerged, but for him the letters remained separate effigies mocking his efforts. Finally he shook his head

200

and let the pages of the book slip from his fingers. 'I'm stalled,' he said.

Marion heard this and smiled at me companionably. 'You have such patience,' she whispered.

I got up to get Samuel and me coffees and those cookies we both loved with the wavy edges and a hole in the middle. Samuel was slipping two on the tips of his fingers when I said 'Let's do something different.'

He gave me a sly look. 'You mean a game?'

I pulled out my newspaper and got a couple of scissors and a tube of paste from the office. Samuel was half asleep when I got back. The morning wore on for him after a late shift on the station.

'You cut out the words you know. Even if you're not sure but you kind of recognize them. Like someone you might have seen once and whose name is just on the tip of your tongue. You cut them out and make sentences.'

He shook his head, but started moving around the page with his fingers.

I was thinking of my game of cutups. Why did it have to be paragraphs from articles, why not just pieces of sentences? Why not just play around with whatever Samuel dropped on the floor? Even those letters which mocked him.

'Makes no sense,' he mumbled to himself.

I thought we were all the time trying to make too much sense, embellishing our words with other words which hung like leaden cloaks from our meaning. Putting together random pieces of text made nonsense, yet seemed to be what we really thought.

Samuel labored beside me with his scissors while I picked up the pieces of newspaper he no longer wanted. I could see he was trying out different combinations. Finally he pasted four words on a page: 'He runs the moon.'

'I wanted "see",' he said, 'but I couldn't find it nowhere.'

I said 'I like it. Let's keep going.' So we cut and pasted our words on paper like good blackmailers.

When I came home, the kitchen was filled with vapors.

201

Carlton was having one of his hour-long showers. I sat down at the table and in the shreds of my newspaper I saw 'Cloud Theft', a farmer in Laos complaining that the Americans had started a monsoon during the Vietnam War by seeding the clouds. Pages later I came upon a little article about frozen tadpoles.

Carlton emerged from the shower as I moved my eyes between clouds and tadpoles. He twisted a beach towel around his lean torso.

'How do you feel?' I asked.

'Spooky. And sparky.' He disappeared into his room.

I thought how much the world made sense now that I could join any two pieces of newspaper. At first they were meaningless, the two paragraphs, the two lines, even words, but it surprised me how with time they could grow towards each other as if some private conversation had begun between them. Carlton could join me in the newspaper game now that he had rid himself of that great galumph of a guy.

Carlton came into the kitchen as I was cutting out the two articles. His hair was combed back into shiny porcupine quills from his lean pale face. He had on his favorite tee shirt, tight black with a meteor crossing his chest. He was all in black down to his snaky trousers and cowboy boots.

I said nothing. He was probably mourning those photos which was natural and perhaps right.

'That poor newspaper,' he said.

Maybe now was the time to tell him of the power he could have by reading with a new alertness.

'It was brave what you did,' I said.

'What?'

'You know. Cutting them up. All those photos.'

He looked a bit shame-faced so I said nothing more but let a little sigh escape.

'Later my mush,' he said. 'Much, much later if I'm lucky.'

'Where you going?'

'To the usual. Scatter myself. The Parrot, the Algiers. Just around.'

Those were Paulo's hangouts.

202

'You know. Just seeing who's lost their tent pegs.'

'But you killed him yesterday.'

'You must understand.' He drew himself up and looked at me with his head to one side like a kindly priest. 'That was only symbolic.'

I was shaking my head like old Samuel. 'You'll be his random boy.'

'Aren't we all?' And then he waved to me before leaving our yellow kitchen, the black shower stall still dripping and me with the shreds and patches of the newspaper on my lap.

If it's just random what happens, if I could just as soon run the moon in Samuel's terms as follow the reasoning of the newspaper's writers, then I've gained nothing from months of abstinence.

I went to bed after that with the newspaper cuttings flung on the floor beside me. Let them talk to each other.

In the morning I discovered that Carlton had never come home. Probably he stayed in Paulo's tiny room. I know that broken-down house he shares with the other Brazilians, the way the doors open all of a sudden into twisted white passageways.

I was late to the Read-to-Read but Samuel sat waiting. 'He didn't want me,' whispered Marion. I began a new reader which I knew was too hard for him. He kept stopping and staring at me. I tried to ignore him, but words began to go round and round my head: 'You'll never learn, never, never, never.' Soon they'd come out of my mouth in a scream.

'What about the game?'

I shook my head at him. 'That was just fooling around.'

'Then I'm a fool maybe.' He gave me a long slow smile.

'Well then,' I said and as I left the room, I pushed the tears right out of my eyes with a hard flick of my finger. I brought back scissors and paste and the newspapers I found by the bin. And those cookies with the holes.

I began to join up the pieces of text Samuel discarded. I played around with them, not bothering to cut away words, just putting his discards together like jigsaws. They were nonsensical, my lines, but I kept going, hoping for meaning. Soon I had a page of newsprint. As I looked down on it I began to pick out messages: 'She has decided to leave the humpbacked whale stranded in a desert of their own making.' 'He that doubts will find the knowing.' And I nodded my head with sage weariness.

Samuel looked over at my work. 'You got a treasure hunt.'

When I came home the shower was pouring down on Carlton. The flat had a burnt smell, and I saw a scorched piece of photo in the sink. I could just make out the darkened remains of Paulo's glowing torso.

I began turning slowly to avoid knocking the table and shower stall. I turned and turned till the room whirled and the moon, tadpoles and stolen clouds turned with me and around me and through me in the yellow kitchen.

ACKNOWLEDGEMENTS

These stories or versions of them were first published in the
following magazines and anthologies:

'The Denver Ophelia' in *Riptide Journal*
'My Red Mustang' in *Lilith Magazine*
'Irony' in *PEN New Fiction*, Quartet Books
'A Spiritual Death' and 'Fairy Godmother' in *Writing Women*
'The Book Thief' in *The Massachusetts Review*
'The Blessing' in *Stand Magazine*
'Man with a Newspaper' first appeared in *North American
Review*
'The Borders of My Self' in *Critical Quarterly*
'Genius' in *The Jewish Quarterly*
'Where Have You Been?' in *Jewish Fiction .net*
'He Runs the Moon' in *The Warwick Review*

I worked on this collection during residencies at the Tyrone
Guthrie Centre in Ireland. I want to thank the wonderful staff
there. Thanks are also due to the Arts Council for a Writers
Award.

I especially want to thank Miriam Hastings who read most
of the stories in this collection. I am grateful for her wise
comments and for her friendship.

Wendy Brandmark is a fiction writer, reviewer and lecturer. She writes both novels and short stories.

Her first novel, *The Angry Gods*, was published by Dewi Lewis in 2003, and the US edition in 2005. Her second novel, *The Stray American*, was published in 2014 by Holland Park Press and was longlisted for the Jerwood Fiction Uncovered Prize 2015.

Wendy's short stories have been widely published in British and American magazines and anthologies. In 2013 she was a fellow at the Virginia Centre for the Creative Arts, and she has had residencies at the Tyrone Guthrie Centre in Ireland in 2014 and 2015.

She has reviewed fiction for a range of magazines and newspapers, including *The Times Literary Supplement, The Literary Review* and *The Independent*.

Wendy has taught creative writing in London for over fifteen years and at present she is a tutor in the Oxford University Master of Studies (MSt) in Creative Writing, and she teaches fiction writing at The City Lit.

She grew up in the Bronx, went to university in Boston and completed her MA in Creative Writing in Denver. London is now her home.

More details are available from

www.wendybrandmark.com
and
www.hollandparkpress.co.uk/brandmark

Holland Park Press is a unique publishing initiative. Its aim is to promote poetry and literary fiction, and find new writers. It specializes in contemporary English fiction and poetry, and translations of Dutch classics. It also gives contemporary Dutch writers the opportunity to be published in Dutch and English.

To

- Learn more about Wendy Brandmark
- Discover other interesting books
- Read our unique Anglo-Dutch magazine
- Find out how to submit your manuscript
- Enter in one of our competitions

Visit www.hollandparkpress.co.uk

Bookshop: http://www.hollandparkpress.co.uk/books.php

Holland Park Press in the social media:

http://www.twitter.com/HollandParkPres
http://www.facebook.com/HollandParkPress
https://www.linkedin.com/company/holland-park-press
http://www.youtube.com/user/HollandParkPress